W9-AOL-451

HAUNTED

SISTER

HAUNTED

SISTER

LAEL LITTKE

HENRY HOLT AND COMPANY   NEW YORK

Henry Holt and Company, Inc., *Publishers since 1866*
115 West 18th Street, New York, New York 10011

Henry Holt is a registered trademark of Henry Holt and Company, LLC

Disributed in Canada by
H. B. Fenn and Company Ltd.

Library of Congress Cataloging-in-Publication Data
Littke, Lael. Haunted sister / by Lael Littke.
p.   cm.
Summary: A sixteen-year-old girl suffers a near-death experience in which her
twin sister, who died in an accident twelve years before, returns to forcibly share
her body. [1. Near-death experiences—Fiction. 2. Twins—Fiction. 3. Sisters—Fiction.
4. Traffic accidents—Fiction. 5. Guilt—Fiction.] I. Title
PZ7.L719Wf 1998 [Fic]—dc21 98-12144

ISBN 0-8050-5729-3 First Edition—1998
Designed by Meredith Baldwin
Printed on acid-free paper in the United States of America. ∞
5 7 9 10 8 6 4

FOR LORI AND DOUG

With special thanks to
Walter D. Hofmann, M.D.,
who helped me understand Lenore

HAUNTED

SISTER

ONE

It was raining on the day I died.

It was a light, gentle rain, just enough to make the trees weep and the flowers bend their heads with its weight. Just enough to make the streets wet and slick.

That's one of the things that caused the accident. That and the man who was in such a hurry to get somewhere that he ran a red light. Then he couldn't get enough traction on the wet street to stop when he saw Scott's car in the intersection.

But I guess the main fault was Scott's. And mine. We were not supposed to be at that intersection at that moment. We were supposed to be in school.

Does it really matter whose fault it was? It happened, and nobody has yet invented a way to make things unhappen.

It all started when Scott caught up to me after our eleven o'clock math class and said, "Hey, Janine, let's cut out and go to the beach."

It wasn't the kind of thing either of us did. But the late-April day was dull and drizzly, and school was a drag on days like that.

"Terrific," I said. "When do we leave?"

To tell the truth, I would have cut school for the whole week if Scott had suggested it. We'd gone out together only a couple of times, even though we'd been in the same schools since fifth grade. It was only recently that we found we liked each other, which surprised me since we're quite different. Scott was always doing things at school. A leader. I'd always been a shy, nonaggressive follower, the kind who blended in with the scenery. A *good* girl. A *boring* girl, except now and then when a flash of recklessness made me do things I wouldn't ordinarily do.

It was one of those flashes that made me say I'd go with Scott to the beach.

"It's raining, you know," he said.

I raised my eyebrows. "So? Is the rain going to make the ocean any wetter?"

Scott grinned. "Should we go now or wait until

after two? I'm supposed to give an oral report in Snyder's class after lunch."

"Are you prepared?"

"No."

"What are we waiting for?"

"Well, well," Scott said. "So you're Lenore today."

"I might be," I admitted.

Scott called me Lenore whenever I bent my usual straight-arrow image a little. I'd told him once I'd been born a twin but that my sister Lenore had died when we were four years old. I had only sketchy memories of her, but I knew she'd been the adventurous, mischievous, sometimes get-into-trouble one. I was the good twin.

I don't remember just when but sometime after she was gone I'd started saying I was Lenore when I did something I knew I shouldn't.

"Okay, Lenore," Scott said, taking my arm. "Let's go. We'll deprive Snyder of my great wisdom and insight today."

"Wait," I protested, as he towed me down the hall. "I have to drop my books off at my locker. I don't think we'll be studying chemistry at the beach."

Pretending to twirl a villain's mustache, Scott gave me a fake leer. "Depends on what kind of chemistry you're talking about, my dear," he said in a gruff voice.

I giggled. Leers weren't Scott's thing, and besides, he hadn't even kissed me yet. I had a feeling it might take place at the beach that very afternoon.

My best friend, Catherine, passed as I was shoving books into my locker.

"Munching today, Janine?" she asked, returning Scott's friendly sock on the arm.

"On a diet." I didn't tell her I was cutting school. That might put her on the spot if one of the teachers asked where I was. "How about tomorrow?"

"Tomorrow it is." Catherine doesn't ask questions.

She gave me a "Go for it" signal with her eyebrows and left.

Slamming my locker shut, I turned to Scott. "Beach, here we come!" I felt free and reckless and not at all like Janine. Today I was Lenore.

We exited the school building and ran through the parking lot in the rain, keeping an eye out for the security aides. We weren't supposed to leave campus without permission, but the rules were eased a little at noon because the food on campus wasn't the greatest. Still, we might be questioned if one of the aides saw us, then we'd have to lie about what we were planning.

Nobody stopped us, and soon we were out on the street in Scott's little blue car, turning south on Sierra Madre Boulevard. Scott flipped on the windshield wipers. They whack-whacked back and forth like fingers wagging at naughty children.

"We'd better pick up some burgers somewhere," Scott said. "Want them now or shall we wait till we get to the beach?"

I thought about sitting somewhere along the ocean in the cozy little car with the rain beating on the roof. I didn't want to be gumming a hamburger while I waited for Scott to move in for that first kiss.

"Let's get them now," I said.

That's why my last thoughts were of ketchup and pickle relish and the greasy smell of french fries. I saw the other car skidding toward us in the rain, but I didn't even have time to scream.

Then I was floating. Not hurt and not scared. Voices came from somewhere. I paid no attention. They had nothing to do with me.

But then one of them yelled, "Clamp! Clamp! I've got a bleeder!" Another one said, "Check that head injury!" Still another said, "I can't get a pulse."

All the while, I floated.

Somebody shouted, "Janine! Janine!" A jolt. Another one that rattled my teeth.

I looked around. I was in a small, pale green room filled with ugly metal equipment. But I was up near the ceiling. It didn't seem to be a problem. A little odd, maybe. I'd never seen a room from that angle before.

Below me I saw a girl lying on a hospital gurney. Bloody. People dressed in baggy green surgical suits mopped at the blood and poked needles into her arms.

The girl wore jeans and a blue denim shirt like I'd put on that morning.

"Why, it's me," I said, then giggled because Miss True, my English teacher, would chide me for not saying, "It is I."

It was me, but then again it wasn't me. I was floating up near the ceiling. I felt fine.

But the girl on the narrow table was a bloody mess.

"Freaky," I commented to myself.

"No respiration," said one of the people standing by the table.

For the first time I realized I was dead.

Dead.

I'd thought it would be different. It should be more dramatic, with maybe trumpets announcing that Janine Palmer was dead. Or maybe violins sobbing in the background, like in the movies.

I'd never thought much about death. Young people don't die. Lenore had died, of course, but that was a long time ago. There'd been that girl in my class when we were in the fourth grade. And little Woody Sinclair down the street who'd been hit by a car last year. But I'd never considered it happening to ME, at least not until I was old like Grandfather Palmer, who was seventy-four when he died.

I was still trying to realize that I was dead when suddenly I felt a pulling, like when Scott towed me through the hall at school. I was going somewhere. I had no choice. There were bright lights and then darkness and I was spiraling through a dark, narrow tunnel. Something bonged, like a giant bell, and there was a whirring and rushing of wind. I thought it would take my breath away— but I had no breath.

I cried out and wondered how I could do that without breathing. I still felt like me, yet I was different.

I was dead.

9

Then the spinning and whirring and bonging stopped. I'd arrived somewhere. I'd come so fast that it took me a while to get oriented.

Dizzily, I looked around. This place was like nothing I'd ever seen before. I can't really describe it because I don't know any words to tell the way it was. There were mists and fogs swirling around me, and I couldn't see clearly.

There were something like tall, graceful buildings in the distance, but their outlines were so blurred I couldn't say for sure that's what they were.

People came. They, too, were not quite like anything I'd seen before. The nearest I can come to describing them is that each one was sort of shimmering.

I recognized several of them. I don't know how. It was just a recognition.

Little Woody Sinclair was there and that classmate of mine who died when we were in the fourth grade. Holly DeWitt, that was her name.

Somebody touched my arm and I turned to see Grandpa Palmer. I remembered him. I'd been almost nine when he died seven years ago.

"Grandpa," I cried. "I'm so glad to see you."

I went to put my arms around him, but he held up his hand. Or at least that was the impression I had.

"Janine," he said. "It's not time for you to be here."

I looked around at the others. I'd thought they all came to welcome me, but they just stood there, silent.

"Well, it wasn't my idea to be here," I said. "Where am I, anyway?"

Grandpa Palmer ignored my question. He spoke gently. "You must go back. You can, you know. But you must hurry."

I shook my head. "How can I go back? I don't know where I am. I don't know how I got here."

"You have the choice," Grandpa Palmer said.

The others nodded solemnly.

I was ticked. I hadn't asked to come. Now they were trying to get rid of me. Go back, they said. How was I to do that? Where was the tunnel I'd come through? Maybe I didn't want to go back. That bloody girl lying on the narrow gurney—did I want to be that girl again?

Maybe I'd rather stay where I was.

"Go back," Grandpa Palmer said urgently, and the others echoed, "Go back." Their eyes were full of love, but they were sending me away.

There was one pair of eyes that held no love. They belonged to a girl who stood to one side watching me. I couldn't read those shimmering eyes. It wasn't hate they held, but I suspected it was the closest thing to it she could feel in this place.

Why was she staring at me?

I realized that looking at her was like gazing into a mirror.

"Lenore?" I asked. "Lenore, is that you?"

She nodded slowly, without speaking.

I felt a rush of joy. This was Lenore, my lost sister, my twin.

"Lenore, I'm so happy to see you," I said. "Aren't you going to say anything to me?"

She spoke now, softly. "You did it, you know. It was your fault."

I was puzzled. "What do you mean?" Her bitterness seemed out of place.

"You took my life."

I backed away, horrified. "Lenore, no. How can you say a thing like that?" My voice choked. "It isn't true."

Lenore's eyes held mine. "You might not re-member now, but you will. Someday when you're back with Dad and Mom and William, you'll remember."

"Back!" I yammered. "I don't know how to go back."

Lenore's voice went on, soft and mesmerizing.

"Back with Boomer and his silly barking and Mrs. Kimberly with her cats next door and the street where you live and the school."

How did she know so much about me? My mind felt stuffed with the things she spoke of. Mom. Dad. William, my eight-year-old brother. I thought of our house and the way the lights shone through the darkness at night and the way it was at breakfast with everybody getting ready to go somewhere.

I thought of school. Of our old dog Boomer.

I thought of Scott.

What had happened to Scott? Did he make it through the accident?

"Is Scott okay?" I asked.

"Go back," Lenore said.

"Back," echoed Grandpa Palmer.

"Back, back, back," the others murmured.

There was too much to leave, back there. I wanted to return.

I had no sooner made my decision when there was darkness again and great, tearing pain that made me cry out.

"Zap her again," a voice said, and a terrible jolt arched my body and flooded me with more pain.

"I'm getting a pulse." The voice sounded excited.

I felt heavy, weighted down, bloated, full of bones and blood and organs. And something else.

"No," I cried out. "You can't come with me!"

But I knew nobody understood.

Except her. Lenore. She was there, crowded into my body with me, crying out with no voice.

"No," I screamed again before I sank down into the heavy blackness of unconsciousness.

TWO

It was more than a week later that I finally surfaced. In the meantime I drifted in some strange world where stars wheeled across purple heavens and phantom music resounded from tall crystal mountains. Other times I heard the ticking of clocks and caught the odors of school corridors filled with students. I saw freeways and firelight and felt the soft touch of a summer rain. Things of the earth. Things that made me want to wake up.

But when I did, there were needles and tubes and pain. The pain tore at me and wrapped itself around me and dug itself into my bones.

I retreated again to that strange world of nowhere.

All the while Lenore was there with me. I don't

know how. She didn't do anything or say anything, but I knew she was there.

Sometimes I heard voices. They called to me. "Janine," they said. "Janine." But I didn't want to answer. I didn't know who they were.

Then there were other voices.

"Janine!" they whispered. "Janine, wake up!"

Familiar. Loving. Pleading. Mom, and sometimes Dad. I wanted to respond, to tell them I was there somewhere in the mists. But I was too tired.

I liked having them there, though. Mom talked to me a lot and sometimes she sang the old songs I liked, the one about the pretty little ponies and another about a ring that had no end. Best of all, I liked it when she stroked my forehead and whispered, "Poor little Janine," the way she used to do when things went wrong in my kid world.

At those times when Mom sang or spoke I could feel Lenore listening. She listened with my ears.

It terrified me that she could do that. Why was she there within me? What did she want?

Once I tried to tell Mom she was there. "Lenore is here," I cried. "She's here with me."

Mom stroked my hand and said, "Don't try to talk, honey. Shhhh. Shhhh. You've been in an accident, sweetheart. I know you're confused, but it will all go away."

I felt Lenore stir nervously.

"Mom, I mean it. I was somewhere—I don't know where—and Lenore . . . Mom, I'm so scared." The speech exhausted me and I slumped.

"Nurse," Mom yelled. She sounded frightened. "Nurse, come quickly. Something's wrong."

The nurse came with a needle and it was crystal mountain time again.

Sometimes, when I came near enough to the surface, I called out for Scott.

"Is Scott all right?" I asked the cool white uniform that stood by the side of my bed.

"Scott is fine. Don't worry about him."

"Is Scott all right?" I cried again, and the calm, firm voice assured me as many times as I asked that "Scott is fine."

But I had a bad feeling about him somewhere in the empty spaces of my pain. What did the cool uniform know about it anyway? Did she even know who Scott was? Wouldn't she tell me he was fine even if he were crushed and broken or even dead? Isn't that what they do in hospitals—keep telling you everything is fine until you get strong enough so they can zap you with the truth?

He couldn't be dead, though. I'd been dead and he hadn't been there, wherever it was I had been.

On the other hand, I didn't know how those

things worked. Maybe he had his own place to go. The fact that I hadn't seen him didn't mean a thing.

"Scott," I wailed. "Scotty."

Then the mists came and I drifted away again to the tall crystal mountains.

Mom was with me when I finally came back for good. She was sitting beside my bed. Not reading or knitting or anything. Just sitting there. Watching me. Behind her I could see white drapes. Somebody had drawn them all around my bed. Was I too awful to see? My left arm was strapped to a board and there was a needle stuck into it, drip-dripping some kind of stuff into my veins. The needle was connected to a tube that came from a bottle hanging on a pole by the side of my bed. There was another tube going into my nose. I was sure there were more of those snaky tubes taking care of my other needs.

There were bandages, too, tight around my chest and head. I could feel them there.

I wasn't your average, everyday beauty queen.

"Mom?" I said.

She was out of that chair as if she'd been ejected from it.

"Janine?" she said softly. "Janine?"

"I'm here, Mom." I wanted to say something flippant, something corny, something to make us both laugh so that things would be back to normal again. But all I could say was "Mom. Mommy. Mommy." Then I started to snivel like a little kid.

Mom put her head down near mine and we cried together. I was tired then, and went back to sleep. This time it was just sleep. No purple heavens. No phantom music. Gratefully I realized that I couldn't even feel Lenore anymore.

Mom was still there when I awoke again. And the white curtains were still around my bed.

"Mom, what happened to me?" I had to know, yet I didn't want to know.

"Janine," Mom said, "you were in a bad accident. You have a head injury, which is what's causing most of your problems." I knew she was telling me the truth.

Or as much of the truth as she knew.

"You're going to be all right," Mom went on. "You're out of the intensive care unit now. Dr. Zeigler was here and she said you're going to be fine. She took some of your tubes away. I called Dad to tell him. He had to make a quick trip out of town, but he'll be back soon. He sends his love."

I thought of all the hours Mom had sat there

while I spun through my alien world and I cried again. It was when I tried to lift my right hand to scrub away my dumb tears that I realized my arm was in a cast. I had been too weak before to lift it. I stared down at it now.

"What else is wrong with me?" I blubbered. Was I hideously hurt?

I wanted to count my arms and legs, but it hurt when I tried to raise my head.

"Nothing that won't mend, honey." Mom stroked my face. "Besides the head injury, you have a broken arm and at least one broken rib and more bruises than you can count."

"Is that all, Mom? I feel so awful. What's wrong with my head? Is my head broken like my arm?"

Her eyes were clear, honest. "Not fractured," she said. "A bad concussion is what you have. It's caused some hallucinations. Your head hit the windshield. That's why it aches so bad."

"Oh," I said. "I thought it was because . . ."

I was going to say "because of Lenore," but I stopped. That would sound like just more hallucinations. I wasn't sure, anyway. Where was Lenore now? Had she gone?

"Because what?" Mom prompted.

"Because of this hard pillow," I said. "It's too fat and it cricks my neck."

"I'll find out if I can bring your own pillow from home," Mom said.

Good old Mom, the comforter, the fixer, always making the bad things go away.

"Mom." Maybe she could make my bad feeling about Scott go away.

She waited. "Yes, honey, what is it?" Worry lines gathered on her forehead.

"I'm scared about Scott, Mom."

Mom's face smoothed. "He's doing all right."

My energy was running out. I wanted to escape into sleep again. But I needed to find out about Scott. "That's what the nurse said. But I feel so scared about him." I licked my lips, wondering where the bad feeling came from. "Tell me the truth. He's hurt, isn't he?"

Mom nodded. "It was a messy accident. Scott's legs were broken and his back is hurt. They had to operate to patch him up."

We were getting closer to the full truth. "Will his legs get better? Will he be able to walk again pretty soon?"

"I'm sure he'll be fine eventually." Mom hesitated only a second before she continued. "Right now he's in a wheelchair, but it's been only nine days since the accident. I'm sure he'll be all right."

I could tell she wasn't sure, and neither was I. I

tried to imagine Scott in a wheelchair. Scott, who managed to be all over the map at once when he was pushing a project or running a student body election or soaring over the high-jump bar at a track meet.

"Mom," I said desperately, "do you think we could see each other? Scott and I? Maybe I'd feel better if I could see him."

"I'll see what I can do." Mom stood up. "I'd better go now so I can pick up Dad at the airport. He'll be here later to see you. I have to go with William to a school event, so I'll see you tomorrow." She fluffed my pillow and gathered up her purse. "Would you like to meet your roommate, Janine? She's anxious to meet you."

I think Mom was trying to get my mind off Scott. I was curious about who was on the other side of that white curtain, but I wasn't ready to meet her.

"I'm really tired," I said. "Maybe tonight when Dad comes."

"Right." Mom came back to give me a peck on the cheek, then left, saying, "William sends his love. He says to tell you he and Boomer really miss you. Anna Mae, too."

Anna Mae was William's eight-year-old play-mate, who was always telling him they were going to get married someday. She already considered herself part of the family.

When Mom was gone, I glued my mind to thoughts of home so I wouldn't think about Scott. I thought about our dog Boomer, and Mrs. Kimberly's cats.

"She's nice."

The words came to me as clearly as if someone had spoken, yet I knew I had heard no voice.

"What?" I said aloud.

"She's nice. Our mother."

Lenore. She *was* still there with me.

This was the first time she'd communicated with me since I'd come back. Since *we* had come back.

It scared me to have her speaking inside my head like that. Intruder! Trespasser!

"Lenore," I said aloud, "you can't stay." I remembered what Mom had said. "You're just a hallucination, anyway."

She laughed softly. *"You know better than that, don't you?"*

I did. I knew Mom didn't really understand. "Whatever you are, you don't belong here any more than I belonged there where you were," I said. "Go back."

That's what they'd said to me, Grandpa Palmer and those other people in that place.

"Get used to it," Lenore answered inside my head. *"I'm staying."*

"You can't," I cried. "This is *my* life. You had your chance. You died."

That was cruel, but it scared me, having her there within me. I wanted her out.

I heard some rustlings on the other side of the white curtain.

"Are you all right, Janine?" The voice was muffled. "Shall I call the nurse?"

I hadn't thought about my roommate hearing me. What must she think?

Pulling myself together, I said, "I'm okay. Guess I drifted off to sleep and was talking to myself."

"Sorry I woke you." The voice sounded apologetic. "Let me know if I can do anything. My name is Hallie."

"Thanks, Hallie. I will." She seemed nice, my roommate. I wondered why her voice was so muffled. What kind of injuries did she have?

Inside my head, Lenore spoke again. *"You don't have to speak out loud, you know. Just talk to me inside your head."*

"If it's my head, what are you doing in it?" I said it inside my head, the way she suggested.

"There, that's the way to do it," Lenore said. *"Sure, it's your head, Janine. But I'm going to*

share it with you now. Maybe we'd better start thinking of it as OUR *head. Although it aches so much that it's not much fun being here."*

"So *why don't you just get out? You can't stay here, Lenore."*

A feeling of sadness overwhelmed me. I knew it came from Lenore.

"Get used to it," she said softly. *"I don't want to fight you, but I'm staying. I just want a chance at life. Can't you understand that? It's beautiful where I was, but it's not life. Nothing is as wonderful as being alive."*

"Headaches and all," I said bitterly.

"Headaches and all," she repeated. *"Think about it. I had only four years of life. Think about all I've missed."*

She was playing on my sympathy. *"I don't want to talk to you right now, Lenore. My head aches."*

"I know."

"Well, then just let me sleep." I was almost too tired to notice that I'd spoken aloud again. A nurse who came through the white drapes at that moment gave me a curious look. But she didn't say anything. It probably wasn't the first time I'd acted strange.

"Time for a bit of a cleanup," the nurse said, setting down a basin. "I think we're going to be getting back to actual food today." She adjusted the bottle of fluid that still dripped into my arm. "The doctor will be in to see you later."

Quickly she wrung out a washcloth that was in the basin and wiped off my face and the hand that wasn't in the cast. The rough, warm cloth felt good.

"I'm so glad we're feeling a little better, Janine," the nurse said. "Maybe tomorrow we'll even get to stand up and take a few steps." Gathering up her equipment, she left, the soles of her white shoes squeaking on the tiles of the floor.

"*And maybe we'll get dizzy and fall flat on our butt,*" Lenore muttered inside my head.

It was so unexpected that I couldn't help but laugh. "*Lenore, where did you learn to talk like that?*"

Lenore sniffed. "*I may be dead, but I'm not totally out of it.*"

I was so drowsy I couldn't concentrate, but I asked, "*How does it work, Lenore? I mean how do you know so much about life when you're dead?*"

Lenore hesitated. "*I can't explain it in terms that you'd understand. But it's something like watching disconnected fragments of TV. Sometimes you can catch glimpses of what's going on, but you can never participate. And you never get to see the whole show."*

She may have said more, but I couldn't follow it. I was fading into sleep and as I let go of my rational thoughts I decided this couldn't really be happening. It was the concussion that was making me weird.

That's all it was, the way Mom had said. When my head got better, the hallucination that was Lenore would go away and I would be myself again, myself as I had known me before the accident.

I slept for a long time and would have slept even longer if someone hadn't touched me on the shoulder. It was my regular nurse again. Mrs. Storch, it said on her nameplate.

"Janine, are you ready for a visitor?" she asked.

I tried to bring myself up from the pit I had been in, a place where voices without bodies spoke to me.

"I don't know," I said. I raised my left hand to check my hair, but encountered only bandages.

"You look fine," Mrs. Storch said. "I wouldn't have awakened you, but I didn't think you'd want to miss this visitor."

She held the drapes open far enough for a wheelchair to roll in next to my bed.

27

Scott! His legs were in casts, propped out straight in front of him on a little shelf. There were bruises over his left eye and a bandage around one wrist. But he was alive!

The aide who pushed his chair lined it up parallel to my bed so we were facing each other. Then she left, saying, "I'll be back in five minutes."

Mrs. Storch let the drapes fall shut and Scott and I were alone.

We hadn't yet said a word. We both wore big silly grins, but I knew they'd melt into tears if we didn't take this slowly.

I reached out my good hand and Scott took it, squeezing gently. We hung on to our grins, but I was scared again. I didn't know whether it was because of that bad feeling I'd had earlier about Scott or because Lenore was reacting as if she had just spotted the world's largest ice-cream cone.

"*Well, well, well,*" she said. "*I'm glad we're finally getting around to something better than needles and headaches.*"

THREE

I remember when I was a kid and swam the length of a pool for the first time. I was scared all the way, but when I was in the deep end where, if I sank, the water would close over my head, I was almost paralyzed with fright. That's the way I felt when Lenore began admiring Scott.

Up until then I'd just been scared and confused and resentful about having her there in my body with me. Now, when I realized what a completely separate person she was, I knew I was in over my head.

I freaked.

"Why don't you just get out of here?" I gritted between clenched teeth. "I don't want you here."

Scott dropped my hand as if it were a rattlesnake. His eyes widened with shock and he grabbed the wheels of his chair.

I'd spoken aloud.

Looking at his hurt, bewildered face was worse than all the bruises and lumps and broken bones I'd discovered since I'd awakened.

"Oh, Scott," I moaned. "Scotty, I didn't mean that."

I wanted to explain, but how could I tell him about Lenore? Besides, there was this big bubble forcing its way through all the passages of my head, growing bigger and bigger until it popped and my whole face was awash with tears.

"I'd forgotten what it was like to burst into tears." Lenore's tone was cool, clinical. *"Quite a sensation."*

Curse her, squatting there somewhere inside me, sampling my misery but completely out of touch with it.

"Keep your comments to yourself." This time I was careful to speak only to her. *"You made me hurt Scott."*

"This is all new to me, you know," Lenore said.

"Then just stay out of it," I told her. *"Go back where you belong."*

I tried to blubber something to Scott, but sobs kept rising up from deep inside me, choking off my voice. Now that I'd started to cry, I couldn't stop.

"Janine," Scott said, taking my hand again. "What's wrong? It's okay. I deserved that."

I shook my head "no" so hard that a sharp pain almost wiped me out.

"Hey," Lenore complained, *"do you have to do that?"*

"Get used to it, Lenore," I said. *"That's pain. Life is full of it."*

I gave my head one more good shake before I stopped, just to hurt Lenore.

"Okay, okay," Lenore said. *"So maybe someday I'll know all about it."*

"Forget someday. Just get out now. Save yourself—and me—a lot of trouble and get out NOW."

Anger had almost overcome my fright.

"I'll take my chances," Lenore said. *"Can't you understand what I've said? I'm staying."*

A new wave of terror nearly swamped me. This *thing* inside me was beyond my control. I couldn't get her out. I felt full, overcrowded, *invaded.* In a way it was like having eaten too much. Except that when you eat too much you know you'll feel better after you've digested it.

Something must have shown on my face because Scott patted my hand, looking as if he might burst into tears himself. I wished I could crawl down into his lap and hug him, but I would've had to drag my IV hookup along with me as well as my arm cast. And besides, where would I sit? Scott's broken legs stuck out in front of him on the platform of the chair, and I didn't think he'd be happy about my sitting on them.

"I'm going to call the nurse, Janine." Scott looked around for the call button.

A woman stuck her head in through the white drapes around my bed. She had a nice face framed by dark hair. "Is there anything I can do to help? I'm Hallie's mother." She looked from me to Scott, then back to me.

"Might as well sell tickets," Lenore muttered. *"We're getting a standing-room-only audience."*

I made a real effort to stay calm. "It's all right," I snuffled. "Thanks, but I don't need the nurse. I'll be okay."

"You're sure?" Hallie's mother took a step toward my bed.

I nodded, careful this time not to shake my head any harder than necessary. "I'm sure. Just give me a minute."

"You okay, Janine?" I guessed that was Hallie's voice from the other side of the curtain. I wondered again why it sounded so muffled.

"I'm just having a good cry," I called back to her between sobs.

"If I can help, just call me," Hallie said as if she could leap to my aid if need be.

"Thanks," I said. "See you later."

"I'd offer you a handkerchief if I had one," Scott said. "Would you settle for a corner of my hospital gown?" He reached under his blue robe and fished out the bottom hem of his skimpy gown.

It looked so ridiculous that I giggled. "Maybe just a Kleenex would do." I motioned toward the box of tissues on my bedside table.

Scott reached for them but couldn't quite make it, so Hallie's mother came and handed me half a dozen. Satisfied then that she had done her part, she went back to Hallie, closing the drapes behind her.

I wiped my eyes with the tissues and honked my nose.

"*Yuck,*" Lenore said as I scrubbed at my nose. "*That's gross.*"

Dropping the slimy tissues into the waste bag pinned to my bed, I said, "*Let me tell you, Lenore, you haven't even begun learning about gross yet.*"

"*I guess I have a lot to look forward to,*" Lenore said sarcastically.

"So leave now," I told her. *"Save yourself the agony."* Giving Scott a shaky smile, I turned my attention to him. "How do I look? Be honest."

Scott grinned. "Like a shipwreck."

"You needn't be *that* honest." Once more I reached for his hand. "Look, what I said when you came in—that wasn't for you. I hope you know that. It was just the tail end of a nightmare. Mom says my brain got scrambled in the accident, and I'm apt to say crazy things for a while."

Scott's grin wobbled. "Maybe it would be better if you did chew me over a little. I deserve it." He looked at my broken arm and the bandages on my head and chest. "I'm sorry I did this to you, Janine. If I hadn't got that bright idea to go to the beach that day, you wouldn't be here."

"You didn't see me refusing, did you? Maybe it was just my day to be clobbered." I tilted my head toward his stretched-out legs. "Anyway, it looks as if you got your share of disaster, too."

Scott shrugged as he looked at his casts. "A temporary problem," he said.

I held up my own cast. "Mine, too. I'll be good as new as soon as they bring me some real food. So don't worry about me."

Scott nodded. "And I'll be in this chair for a while, but I promise to take you to the Homecoming Dance in the fall. I'll be ready to dance all night by then."

We smiled at one another, and I knew that Scott wasn't telling the whole truth any more than I was.

Scott's nurse came and wheeled him away then.

"See you later," he called as he rolled out of my room.

"*The sooner the better,*" Lenore said inside my head.

I didn't answer. I was tired and closed my eyes.

"*I was hoping he'd kiss us,*" Lenore said.

That fried me. "*What do you mean 'us'? If he'd kissed anybody, it would have been* me. *He doesn't know anything about you.*"

Lenore laughed. "*I would get the benefits. I feel whatever you feel, physically.*"

"*Then feel sleepy and turn out your lights.*"

Lenore was silent for a moment. "*Has Scott ever kissed you?*"

"*I thought you knew everything,*" I muttered.

"*No,*" Lenore said softly. "*Not at all.*"

"*Well, let it be a mystery then.*" I prepared to sleep, but I was uneasy. My head and arm made me uncomfortable. So did Lenore. Having her there within me was like being in an overcrowded elevator with no room to move.

Lenore wasn't ready to sleep. *"When will we see Scott again?"*

The panic returned. *"Look,"* I said. *"He's my friend. You keep your claws off him."*

Lenore laughed. *"Aren't you forgetting something, sister dear? I can't do anything you don't do."*

I thought about it. What Lenore said was true. Even though she was a separate personality, she was within *my* body. She couldn't do anything I didn't want to do.

I *was* in control.

The panic ebbed a little and I slept.

I don't know how long I was asleep, but I awakened to hear Lenore telling me to open my eyes.

"Something's going on," she said. *"I want to see."*

I opened my eyes and saw a doctor I recognized.

"Hello, Janine," she said. "Remember me?"

Her nameplate said Dr. Zeigler. She was the one Mom had mentioned, and I knew I had seen her face in the mists I'd floated in during my out time.

"I think so," I said. "But I can't remember much else about you."

"Not to worry," Dr. Zeigler said. "We'll have plenty of time to get acquainted. How's the headache?"

"Bad."

"Give it a couple of weeks," Dr. Zeigler said. "It'll improve."

Inside my head, Lenore groaned.

"You got a real bash on the head, among other things," Dr. Zeigler continued. "It made Jell-O of your brain for the time being."

That was a good description. "Is it really going to get better?"

"The body is a wonderful mechanism," the doctor said.

I noticed she didn't really say yes or no to my question.

"What other things?" I asked. "I mean, you said, 'a bash on the head, among other things.'"

"Want it in medical terms or plain English?" Dr. Zeigler unwrapped my left arm from the board it had been attached to, and a nurse took all the IV stuff away.

"I haven't been to med school yet," I said. "So you'd better make it plain English. On the other hand, I got a C in English last semester. Maybe you should draw a picture."

37

Dr. Zeigler laughed as she examined my head bandages. "You're an okay girl, Janine. Did you know you're going to get a real treat today? A taste of actual food, instead of the intravenous stuff. At least we'll find out if you can tolerate real food."

"I've forgotten how to chew."

"It will all come back." Finished with her examination, Dr. Zeigler sat on a chair by my bed. "Now, about what happened to you. Did you know we thought we'd lost you? You gave us a real scare there for a while."

I didn't know how to answer. Could I tell her that I really had been dead but had chosen to come back? I had the feeling she'd be able to handle it. Maybe I could tell her about Lenore.

I could feel Lenore inside me. Watching. Listening. What would she do if I told somebody about her?

"How'd you get me back?" I asked Dr. Zeigler.

"Well," she said, "I'm sure you've seen hospital shows on TV where they put paddles on somebody's chest and zap them with electricity so the heart will return to its normal rhythm. We did that to you. For a while we thought you weren't coming back."

"I felt the jolts," I said.

Dr. Zeigler nodded. "You have some chest injuries as well as the head trauma. You also lost a lot of blood, and we had to pour in a whole new batch."

I smiled. "I sure caused you a lot of trouble."

"All in a day's work," she said. "Look, I think I will draw you a picture, sort of. I'll bring your X rays, if you're interested, and show you what happened."

X rays! Would they show Lenore inside of me? Would there be a funny shadow on the film along with my bones and all the pulsing and flowing things that make up my body? If Dr. Zeigler looked at it and said, "There's something strange here," that would be the time to tell about Lenore because then they would have to believe me.

I could wait.

"I'd love to see my X rays," I said.

"Good." Dr. Zeigler stood up. "Now I'm going to introduce you to your roommate." She drew the white drapes back, running it along its track so that it was like a curtain opening and I was there onstage.

"Okay, Hallie, here she is," she said to the girl in the other bed. "Janine, this is Hallie. She knows you pretty well already since she helped us watch you while you were asleep."

Hallie smiled at me. She had pretty dark hair like her mother, but that was all I could tell about her looks. Her face was a rainbow of healing bruises. A bandage came down over one eye and there were stitch scars along one cheek and across her lips. When she smiled, I caught the gleam of wires.

"My jaws are wired shut," she said. "You'll have to forgive me if I'm mush-mouthed."

Now I knew why her voice had sounded muffled.

"I will if you'll forgive me for talking in my sleep." I needed to give her some explanation for why she'd heard me speaking aloud before I learned to talk to Lenore inside my head.

"And if you'll forgive *me,* I have to go see patients who really need me," Dr. Zeigler said. "You girls have fun getting acquainted."

"If you can't find us, you'll know we went out for a movie," Hallie said. "Maybe we'll pick up some guys and head for MacDonald's."

"Pick up one for me and I'll join you," Dr. Zeigler said as she left.

"*I like Hallie,*" Lenore said inside my head. "*She's my first friend.*"

I shivered. I was swimming again and knew I was in the deep end of the pool.

FOUR

Reminding myself again that I, not Lenore, was in control, I said, "What happened to you, Hallie?"

It sounded rude and abrupt, but I had to get my thoughts away from Lenore.

Hallie didn't seem to mind the change of subject.

"Car accident," she said through her wired-shut teeth. "Same as you. Except mine was my own fault. Thought I was a better driver than I am."

Although her speech was slurred, I could understand her if I listened closely. "How do you mean the accident was your fault? Or am I asking too many questions?"

"Ask all you want, Janine. I'm just glad you're finally awake." She flashed me a metallic smile.

"My parents gave me a cool little car for my sixteenth birthday and I piled it up. Nobody to blame but myself."

I could feel Lenore listening with interest.

To Hallie I said, "You must have been here in the hospital for quite a while if you watched my entire Sleeping Beauty act."

She nodded. "My main problem is this." She pulled back the sheet and I saw that she was in a full body cast. "My back is messed up and a lot of other stuff. Guess I should feel lucky to be here at all." Her voice dropped. "Or maybe not."

"Well." I searched for something cheerful to say. "Well, think of the celebration when you finally get to go home."

It sounded dumb. I wished I hadn't said it.

Hallie turned to look out the window. "It would be a bigger celebration if Kevin would come home. He's my boyfriend. He left on a trip to Hawaii the day before this happened and I haven't seen him since."

What kind of a jerk wouldn't fly home to see his girl when she was so badly injured? "I guess he keeps the post office busy, though," I said.

When Hallie turned back, her face was sad. "Kevin's not much for writing. I try to write to *him* every day, but what is there to say about a hospital room?" Scrapping the sad look, she gave me another tinny smile. "The guy who came to see you, is he somebody special?"

"Kind of," I admitted. "It's his fault that I'm here."

The words came out before I could stop them. I hadn't meant to say that, but it was a relief to have it said. It *was* Scott's fault. If he hadn't asked me to go to the beach, neither one of us would be there in the hospital.

That wasn't fair. Accidents happen. Anytime. Anyplace. To anyone. Why did I feel it was necessary to assign blame?

"I don't mean that," I said. "Scott couldn't help it. I don't hold it against him."

But did I? If it hadn't been for him, I wouldn't have Lenore there with me now, blaming me for causing her death.

Just then the dinner cart arrived. My tray contained several mounds of unrecognizable soft food and some red Jell-O. Hallie got a tall container of pinkish liquid, complete with a straw so she could drink it between her wired-shut teeth.

I scooped up some of the Jell-O with a spoon and put it into my mouth. It tasted good. It sure beat the IV or the nose tube.

"*Hey,*" Lenore said. "*This is great stuff.*"

43

I was feeling mellow now that my life was getting back to some of the things I recognized. Lenore might be there sharing my space, but *I* was in control. I could afford a few nice words to her. She was, after all, my sister—my twin. Why not let her feel a little of what life was like?

"*This is just hospital food,*" I told her. "*Wait until I treat you to a meal of major junk food. A cardboard hamburger and a bag of greasy french fries. Then you'll know what* real *living is.*"

"*Let's go for it!*" Lenore sounded eager.

"Hallie." I waved my spoon. "When we get out of here, let's head straight for the Golden Arches. Cheeseburger, fries, the works!"

Hallie groaned. "Heaven on earth! Throw in a hot fudge sundae with nuts and it's a date."

I was scooping up more Jell-O when Dad strolled into the room. His blue pinstriped suit was rumpled as if he'd just got off the airplane from that business trip Mom had told me about.

"Hi, honey," he said, striding across the room to kiss me on the forehead. "How's my girl?"

Tears sprang into my eyes. "Dad." I dropped my spoon and reached out to him. I wanted to feel his big hands around mine, those hands that had fixed broken dolls and wagons and little-girl dreams when I was small. I choked up. "I'm so glad to see you."

"I was here almost every day while you were sleeping, Janny." He pulled up a chair and sat close to my bed. "Wouldn't you know you'd wake up while I was out of town?"

"It's all right. You're here now." I loved having him near. He was big and warm and smelled of airplane. Reaching for his hand, I said, "Where was it you had to go?"

"To Idaho on business. I visited Grandma Palmer while I was there. She told me you'd be all right."

"How did Grandma know I'd be all right?"

Dad hunched over my hand as if it were a crystal ball. "The ancient ones know all," he intoned. Straightening up, he said, "I don't know how she knew. She told me on the day we drove out to the cemetery to visit Grandpa's grave."

"Maybe *he* told her," I said.

Dad smiled. "Well, if anybody could send a message from beyond the grave, your grandfather could. I guess you don't remember him very well, do you?"

What would Dad say if I told him I had recently seen Grandpa in that strange place I'd gone to? "Sure, I remember him. He and Grandma came here to California to visit us the year before he died. I guess that's the only time I saw him, except when we all went to Idaho. But I can't remember that trip."

"*Yes, you can,*" Lenore said. "*That's when you took my life.*"

"No." I shook my head. "I can't remember that."

"Of course not." Dad gave me an odd look, and I realized I'd said the same thing twice.

"*You'll remember soon,*" Lenore insisted. "*Ask Dad about that trip.*"

"*Stop butting in, Lenore. This is between Dad and me.*"

"*He's my dad, too,*" she said. "*Remember? Now ask him.*"

I wanted to resist her, but I needed to find out. "Dad. That time we all went to Idaho. That was when Lenore died, wasn't it?"

"Yes. But you wouldn't remember that, either. You were only four."

"No." I shook my head again. "I don't remember."

"*Think,*" Lenore prodded. "*It's there. In your memory.*"

"Dad, how did she die?" I asked. "Lenore, I mean."

"You know how she died. We've told you before."

"Tell me again."

Dad hesitated. "It's not something I like to talk about, honey."

I gripped his hand, wanting to tell him I had to know because of Lenore.

But wouldn't it be better if I waited until I saw Dr. Zeigler's X rays before I started insisting that Lenore was there with me? There might be proof.

I relaxed my grip. "She drowned," I said. "In Grandpa's pond."

They'd told me that. I didn't remember it. Not at all.

Dad nodded slowly. "It was a terrible accident."

"My death was no accident," Lenore insisted.

"It wasn't my fault," I said. "I didn't do it. I can't remember. I can't remember. I can't remember." I couldn't stop my voice from rising.

Dad looked alarmed. He leaped to his feet. Hallie must have pushed the call button because Mrs. Storch came running. She brought a needle to poke into my arm, and soon I sank into darkness. But before I did, I heard Lenore say, *"You can forget about it for now, but sometime soon it will all come back."*

There were a couple of bad days after that. I

drifted again and babbled. In the few lucid moments I had, I hoped Lenore would get tired of the needles and tubes and throbbing pain so that she'd go back where she belonged, wherever that was. She was my sister, yes, but it wasn't right that she was intruding into my space. I wanted her out. I wanted to go back to being good, familiar Janine.

But I underestimated the strength of her determination to stay. She stuck with me even though my cast had to be removed, sores underneath treated and cleaned, then the cast replaced. She was there even though my head boomed with pain.

Lenore stayed, crowding my space, sharing my pain. Sometimes when I woke up, especially after an injection of pain medication, I could feel Lenore poking around in my mind as if she were trying to get into my thoughts and memories. At those times I screamed and babbled, which scared Hallie so that she called Mrs. Storch, and that usually brought more needles.

Gradually I began to feel a little better, but the days were long. Mom came each day with messages from William, and Dad popped in whenever he could. My best friend, Catherine, came every few days with news of school, and Hallie was always there.

I received almost daily notes from Scott. I liked them, but I wished he'd come again in person.

One day Dr. Zeigler brought my X rays for me to look at, as she'd promised.

She held one of them up to the light. I saw that it was a picture of my chest, with ribs curving around in graceful patterns.

"Here's the broken one." She pointed at a rib that didn't fit the pattern. "When you move around, it shifts and that's what jabs you."

Eagerly I scanned the film, trying to see some evidence of Lenore in there among the shadows of bones and organs. But I didn't know what was supposed to be there and what wasn't.

Dr. Zeigler showed me the pictures of my head and arm, too.

There wasn't anything at all that might reveal Lenore's presence.

I was weak with disappointment. How could I say anything about her unless there was some proof of her existence? If I started babbling about her, Dr. Zeigler would probably call in the shrinks and I'd be toted off to some psychiatric ward where I'd spend the rest of forever.

"You're really anxious to go home, aren't you?" Dr. Zeigler asked.

My heart thudded. My vibes were getting through to her.

"Dr. Zeigler," I said. "There's something I need to tell you."

"About Lenore?" she said.

I almost choked. "Yes. How did you know?"

"You talk about her when you're asleep," she said. "Your mother told me you had a twin who died."

She knew! Swimming in relief, I reached out to clutch her hand.

Dr. Zeigler pulled up a chair and sat down by my bed. "Janine," she said, "I know you think Lenore returned with you. But this is what really happened. Your head injury has caused your personality to fragment. You've heard of multiple personalities, haven't you?"

Was she denying Lenore's existence now? "Yes," I said. "I've seen movies about stuff like that."

Dr. Zeigler nodded. "The death of your twin was a terrible trauma all those years ago. When you whacked your head, it stirred up a lot of things, and for some reason a new personality appeared to take care of things you don't want to face."

"Like what?" I asked.

50

Dr. Zeigler smiled. "Perhaps we can find out. But I truly believe that what you think is your dead twin is just another side of your own personality."

"But, but," I sputtered. "But she tells me little things about the place where she's been. The place I went to after the accident. She tells me about how she catches glimpses of my life but can never see the whole thing."

"The mind is a wonderful thing," Dr. Zeigler said. "When there's no explanation for something, it supplies one."

"So I'm just making that up myself?"

"Not consciously," she answered. "It's very complex. However, I can assure you that Lenore is not here with you."

I wished I could believe her. But she didn't have a clue. She was falling back on what she'd learned in medical school.

"Multiple personality is not an uncommon occurrence," Dr. Zeigler continued. "We think you'll reintegrate as your injuries heal and you get stronger. If not, we'll call in a psychiatrist for an evaluation."

Yeah. Right. And off to the funny farm I'd go.

Dr. Zeigler stood up. "Hang in there, Janine.

Things are going to get better, I promise." She started toward the door, then turned back. "By the way, we'll be getting you on your feet this afternoon. As soon as you can walk, we'll release you to go home."

She left.

I expected Lenore to say something, to jeer at the doctor's theory or reemphasize her own presence. But she was quiet, and I went to sleep.

Mrs. Storch came in after lunch to get me up. She didn't waste any time. Putting an arm behind my shoulders, she eased me to a full sitting position, being careful about my broken rib, and told me to swing my legs over the side of the bed. My head spun, but she supported me, assuring me things would settle down soon. Then she half lifted me to a standing position.

I'd thought walking would be merely a matter of getting on my feet and taking one step after another, the way it had always been. But now I didn't think I could even move my feet. My broken rib jabbed into something and my broken arm hung from my shoulder like a ton of iron.

"Keep your back straight," Mrs. Storch instructed. "Then your ribs won't hurt so much."

I panted, "I'm going to pass out."

"I'll catch you." Mrs. Storch had no sympathy.

The blood was deserting my head. I was going to barf. Or faint. Or both.

"You have to get some exercise," Mrs. Storch insisted.

"I hate this," Lenore said. *"I didn't know it would be this bad."*

Suddenly I was glad for the pain, grateful for the nausea. *"It's going to get worse, Lenore. You haven't seen anything yet."* It would all be worth it if it would dislodge Lenore.

"Will it help us get out of the hospital?" Lenore asked. *"This exercise?"*

"It's the only way," I said.

After an eternity and a half, Mrs. Storch let me get back into bed.

"Pretty bad, huh?" she said. "I'm going to give you some exercises you can do in bed. The more you do, the faster you'll get out of this torture chamber."

She showed me how to lift and flex my good arm and then how to move my legs around. "I want you to do these things every time you think about it," she told me.

I was glad when she finally left. Drenched with

sweat, I just wanted to go to sleep and forget the pain, forget the accident, forget all that was ahead until I would feel like myself again. Forget Lenore, who had been quiet while Mrs. Storch was demonstrating the exercises. I wondered if she had fainted. Could she do that?

I drifted off to sleep, thinking about being back in school again, only I had to struggle to move along the corridors, concentrating on how to make my body work. It was an uneasy sleep. I kept dreaming of moving my legs and raising my left arm the way Mrs. Storch had told me. Up, around, and down. Up, around, and down.

But I wasn't dreaming. My arm *was* moving.

That's funny, I thought. *Had Mrs. Storch come back while I slept? Was she moving my arm for me?*

Then I knew what was happening. Lenore was moving my arm. She was slow and awkward about it because she didn't remember how to operate a body.

But now she was learning how to operate *my* body.

I was no longer in total control.

FIVE

The thought of Lenore being able to move my arm terrified me. I started screaming. I tried to say, "Get her away from me," but my tongue and lips wouldn't form the words. What came out was gibberish, as if Lenore were trying to speak for me as well as move my arm.

Hallie woke up and hit the call button. Mrs. Storch came on a trot. By that time I was flopping around, yammering that Lenore was the one moving my body.

Mrs. Storch yelled for an aide to come help hold me down. The next thing I knew I was fighting my way up through layers of blackness that hung on to my body like heavy cobwebs.

Mom and Dad stood by my bed, watching me.

"What happened?" I asked before the memories came back.

"Honey." Mom coughed the way people do when they have bad news to say and don't quite know how to get started.

"Janine." Evidently Dad decided to have a go at it. "You had some kind of seizure." Then he hurried on in the kind of voice you imagine airline pilots using to reassure their passengers that "everything is just fine, folks," right when the plane is spiraling toward the earth at six hundred miles per hour. "It's nothing to worry about, Janny. Lots of people with head injuries go through this sort of thing."

Inside my head, Lenore snorted, almost setting me to screaming again. But I didn't want another needle.

"The doctors want to do another brain scan," Dad continued.

"Another?" I said. "When did they do the first one?"

"Right after the accident. It didn't show much of anything. They want to do another just as a precaution, to see if anything new shows up." He tried on a smile, but it didn't fit well and he took it off again. "Can you talk, Janine?"

"Sure I can talk. Why wouldn't I be able to talk?"

Mom and Dad looked relieved.

"Just checking." Mom smoothed my hair, or at least the part of it that wasn't covered by my head bandage. "Hallie said you were talking in your sleep before the seizure but that the words didn't make sense. Sometimes speech patterns get all scrambled from your kind of injury. I guess you were having a nightmare."

Not a nightmare. Lenore.

Inside my head, fury sparred briefly with terror and won.

"*LENORE!*" I thundered.

She didn't answer, but I knew she was there somewhere, watching through my eyes, hearing with my ears, smirking to herself with the knowledge that she could move my arm and make sounds with my vocal cords.

"*LENORE!*" I demanded.

Still no response. She was hiding from me, somewhere in the folds and creases and pulsating cells of my brain, like a naughty child caught fiddling around with the family car.

"Are you all right, Janine?" Mom bent over me, touching my face, alarmed that I was going off into something ugly again.

"I'm all right, Mom." Silently I promised Lenore that I would deal with her later. "How soon can they do the brain scan?"

I didn't have any great hopes that anything would show up. Very likely there would be no blips or seismographic vibrations on a chart to show that Lenore was there with me. But there would also be nothing to show I'd had a seizure. I was not afraid of a brain scan.

Besides, I wanted Lenore to know I was after her.

The scan was done that afternoon and showed nothing abnormal. Dr. Zeigler came to tell me I'd had an accident-related seizure but not to worry about it.

Lenore stayed in hiding until the next day when I was allowed to go visit Scott, transported in a wheelchair pushed by a nurse's aide, who cheerfully filled me in on all the happenings on my floor as we rolled along.

"Room 212 died last night," she said. "One minute she was, y'know, eating her dinner, happy as a clam, and the next minute all these, y'know, alarms went off, and after a while they came hauling her out all, y'know, wrapped in a sheet from head to toesies. Room 235 is new. He fell out of a tree and hasn't, y'know, woken up yet. Room 247 . . ."

"How long have you worked here?" I interrupted her litany of catastrophes. What had she broadcast about me after the incident the day before? "Room 227 really, y'know, freaked out," I could almost hear her saying. "Just like something out of, y'know, *Exorcist II* or something."

"I'm here two months tomorrow," she answered. "I came the day Room 289 tried to, y'know, off himself with a butter knife from his dinner tray. I had to, y'know, help clean up and . . ."

"Well, well, here we are already," I announced loudly as soon as I spotted Scott's door. Room 502. His little world within this wider world of broken bodies.

The nurse's aide wheeled me into the room, twirling the chair so that it came to rest alongside Scott's bed with us facing each other.

"I'll be back in, y'know, fifteen minutes," the aide said. "I have to go check on Room 244. A motorcycle case. Almost scraped an ear off when he met the, y'know, pavement." She waved cheerfully and left.

Scott grinned. "Who wound her up?"

I grinned back. "I think she runs on solar power."

He reached for my hand. "Janine, I'm so glad you came."

"Scott," a voice said, "if you want a little privacy, I'll close your curtain."

I had eyes only for Scott when I came into the room, but now I saw he had a roommate who sat in a chair by the window, reading. As he spoke, he stood up. It was Rafe Belmont, known as The Hunk at our high school. He had a reputation for loving and leaving.

"Oh, it's you, Janine." Rafe got up from his chair and walked over to grasp my hand. "So maybe I *won't* close the curtain."

He grinned down at me, his dark eyes snapping sparks.

I quivered a little when he touched my hand, just like any freshman girl with a crush on the local heartbreak hero. And just like any freshman girl, I looked up at him through my lashes and gave him a come-up-and-see-me-sometime smile.

Right there in front of Scott.

What was the matter with me?

"*Well,*" Lenore said. "*Things are getting better and better.*"

Lenore. It was Lenore who had given him that flirtatious smile—with my face.

Panic smacked me, but I kept my voice steady. *"Forget it. He's not your type."*

"Speak for yourself, Janine. This one's for me."

"No way. Forget you ever met him, Lenore."

"Hey, Rafe," Scott said. "You can let go of my girl's hand now. And please *do* pull the curtain closed as you go."

"I'm being kicked out," Rafe said cheerfully. He placed my hand back in my lap. "Come again *soon,* Janine."

Struggling to stay in control over Lenore, I said, "I didn't even know you were in the hospital, Rafe."

"Guess it happened when you were taking your long winter's nap." Apparently he knew all about my case. "I just had a little knee operation. Football injury. They'll be turning me loose any day now."

"He rubs that in twenty times a day," Scott fake-complained. "Says if I'm on good behavior, they'll spring me, too."

With a wave at Scott and a burning look at me, Rafe pulled the curtain around Scott's bed and went back to his own.

61

As soon as we were alone, Scott reached for my hand again. I looked at him stretched out there on his bed with his two heavy leg casts attached to cables that kept them suspended in midair. This wasn't the way Scott should be spending his time.

This wasn't the way I should be spending mine, either.

"I hate it here, Scott," I said.

"Who doesn't? But you should be getting out pretty soon."

"How about you?"

"Oh, they like me so well they're going to treat me to another operation."

"Another one? What's left to fix?"

"Seems as if everything is disconnected." Scott grinned as he said it, but the bad feeling I'd had about him returned. To get away from it I said, "I wish we could finish our trip to the beach."

Still grinning, Scott nodded. "Okay, Lenore. When do we leave?"

I could feel Lenore come to full attention.

"Lenore?" she said. *"He called you Lenore. Have you told him about me?"*

I was exasperated. *"When do you think I could have done that? You monitor everything I say."*

"But why did he say my name then?"

"It's because I told him once that I always blamed you for the bad things I did when I was lit-

tle. So now when I do anything daring, he calls me Lenore."

"*You call yourself Lenore only when you feel guilty about something.*" Lenore's voice held a note of triumph. "*What does that tell you?*"

Why didn't she stop badgering me? "Just shut up," I yelled. "I'm *not* Lenore and never have been!"

As I watched Scott's face crumple, I realized I'd done it again. I'd spoken aloud.

It took me a long time to convince Scott that I hadn't meant what he'd heard me say. I told him my head was unwired and sometimes my words didn't come out right. I told him I was sorry.

He said it was okay. But I knew it wasn't.

By the time I got back to my room, I was exhausted.

"*Lenore,*" I said as soon as I was in my bed. "*You make me crazy. I can't tolerate you any longer.*"

"*You're not blaming that scene with Scott on me, are you?*"

"*Yes, I am. I wouldn't have said what I did if you hadn't kept hacking at me.*"

"*How do you know?*" Lenore asked. "*You do blame him for putting you in this condition.*"

63

"You're always talking about blame and whose fault everything is, Lenore. Accidents happen."

"Why do you keep saying that what happened to me was an accident?"

"Look, get off it! You're like somebody who wants to play a tune but can hit only one note." I felt my face flushing and I had to concentrate on not speaking out loud. "If you keep messing around with my machinery, moving my arms and smiling with my lips and saying words I don't want to say, I'll tell somebody about you. Somebody will know how to get rid of you."

"If you start talking too much about me, they'll clap you in the psycho ward for sure."

"That's true. And guess who'll be right there with me. You'll never see the world outside of this hospital if you don't lay off, Lenore. Think about it."

I guess she thought about it because there were no more nightmares with me shouting gibberish and there were no more attempts by her to do my exercises.

Oh, those exercises. They hurt, and I wanted to forget them. But I could feel my body getting stronger, so I pushed myself. The effort paid off. It was less than a week after my confrontation with Lenore that Dr. Zeigler told me I was ready to go home.

They made me leave the hospital in a wheel-chair even though I could walk with only slight dizziness by then. But they said it was hospital policy to escort patients to the front door on wheels.

The nurse's aide with the long-play mouth came to push my chair.

"Do you want to, y'know, take a little detour?" she asked as we left my room after saying good-bye to Hallie. Mom and Dad were there with me, hovering over my chair, carrying my suitcase, worrying about my medication.

I looked up at them. "Can you spare five minutes?"

"Sure," Dad said. "Go ahead and see Scott. We'll wait for you at the front door."

The nurse's aide hung a sharp left. "I'm going to, y'know, miss you," she said as we rolled into the elevator and she pressed the button for the fifth floor. "I guess your roommate will, too."

"Hallie will be going home soon, too," I said.

The nurse's aide shook her head. "Not that one. It's going to be a stack of Sundays before she gets out of here."

I twisted my head so I could look at her. "Hallie? I understood she'd be leaving as soon as her jaws heal."

"Well, she won't." The aide was as cheerful as always.

"But we made a date," I insisted, as if that should make a difference. "We're going to go have a burger and stuff as soon as she can chew."

The elevator stopped smoothly at the fifth floor and we rolled out into the corridor. "Better tell your tastebuds to, y'know, cool it."

I wanted to question her further, but we were at Scott's room then. Besides, what did she know? She was obsessed with gloomy stuff. Probably made half of it up.

Scott was sitting up this time, his legs straight out in front of him. He and Rafe were playing chess.

"This is my lucky day," Rafe said. "I'll squeeze into that chair and escape with you."

Tossing my head, I smiled. "If you can fit, come on."

I couldn't believe I'd said that. But it had to have been me. Lenore could manage only gibberish, except inside my head.

"Forget it, Rafe," Scott said. "You're not squeezing into any chair with my girl." He seemed to have forgiven me for the blunder I made the last time I'd been there.

"Well, that's okay," Rafe said. "Think how disappointed the nurses would be if I left."

I wasn't in the mood for their kidding. I was scared about the way I'd reacted to Rafe. And even more, I was feeling scared about going home. I mean, what if something happened there? Here at the hospital there were people who came running whenever I pressed the call button. And how would my room at home look to me now? I felt like a different person from the Janine who had last seen it.

And what about Lenore?

"I came to have you guys autograph my cast," I said.

"Glad to oblige." Rafe found a pen and signed my cast with a flourish.

"I'll put down the phone number here, too," Scott said as he wrote his name. "Call me when you're settled." He fiddled with the pen, not looking at me. "They're doing my operation tomorrow."

I could tell he was nervous about it. "I'll be thinking about you."

He reached out to squeeze my hand. "Thanks, Janine."

I don't know if he meant to say any more. Maybe he didn't want to say it in front of Rafe.

As for me, I wanted to lean in toward the bed and kiss him good-bye. But I was shy about doing that with Rafe there.

Besides, I didn't want to share that first kiss with Lenore.

Pasadena looked sun-drenched and every house seemed to sport azaleas and camellias in full bloom as we drove home. I was happy to be out again, away from the prisonlike walls of the hospital.

Physically, our house looked the same from the outside. I didn't know what I expected. It had been only a month since I'd been there.

Maybe it just felt different to me emotionally because I knew Lenore was looking at it, too.

"Home sweet home," she said as Dad stopped the car in the driveway. *"Or it would have been."* She sounded wistful.

What could I say? She was right. It would have been her home as much as mine if she had lived. We would have shared a room. We would have giggled secrets to each other in the darkness of the night.

Suddenly, I was overwhelmed with a feeling of loss.

"I wish you had lived, Lenore." I meant it.

I waited for her to say, *"I would have if it hadn't been for you."* But she didn't say anything.

"Look," I said. *"If I let you stay here with me for a while without telling anybody about you, maybe for a month or so, will you promise not to make any trouble?"*

I could almost feel her smile. *"And if I do, then what?"*

"Then you'll leave at the end of the agreed time. Get out of my life."

"Not much of a bargain from my point of view."

What was the use of trying to reason with her?

Mom and Dad mother-henned me into the house, clucking about how I should go right to bed after lunch.

Inside, everything was familiar and very dear to me since I'd almost lost it. There was Mom's big cedar chest in the entry hall with the mail basket on it and the big mirror above it. Off to the left was the living room with its earth-tone colors and comfortable furniture.

All of a sudden, William burst through the front door. I assumed he'd been over to Anna Mae's house, or maybe his friend David's, while Mom and Dad came after me.

"Janine, is that you?" he said as he ran toward me.

"Who else would it be?" I held out the hand that wasn't in the cast.

I could feel Lenore watching through my eyes. *"So this is our little brother,"* she said.

William thudded to a stop in front of me. He looked up, and the happy grin slid slowly from his face to be replaced by a puzzled frown. Turning his head a little, he squinted at me.

"Janine," he said again. "Is that *really* you?"

SIX

Did William know? Could he tell that Lenore was there, crowded into my body with me? He was a kid. Didn't kids and animals sense things that adults couldn't see?

Oh, blessed William. Perhaps he could be a witness when the time came for me to prove Lenore was there with me and that I wasn't just a multiple personality as Dr. Zeigler had said.

I felt like singing. I felt like skipping around the room, yelping that I had an ally, someone who would back me up when I told my unbelievable story.

Was this the time to do it? Should I blurt it out right then and there, asking William to verify what I was saying?

"What are you going to do?" Lenore asked uneasily.

"Maybe I'll introduce you to our folks."

She laughed. *"Go ahead. Maybe they'd like to meet me."*

I hadn't thought about that. How would Mom and Dad react if I could convince them that Lenore really was there with me? After all, Lenore was their child, just as much as I was. They'd loved her during the brief years she'd lived, and they'd grieved when she died. Would they want to keep her there with us at any cost, even if it meant I must share my life, my body, with her?

"They don't want to meet you this way," I said.

"Try them. Let's find out."

I stood there looking at William like an actress who has forgotten her lines. Mom and Dad—the audience—watched.

William, who had delivered his speech, waited. Like an expanding accordion, the silence stretched out to its widest limits. I had the impression that soon it would start closing and squeeze screams from my throat.

Taking a step toward William, I put my good arm around him. "Sure, it's Janine. Who did you think it would be? The Queen of England?"

He pulled away, but I'd expected him to do that. William doesn't take to hugging. He continued to squint up at me without saying anything.

I didn't want him to say any more until I had a chance to talk to him alone.

I pointed to my plaster-encased right arm. "William, would you like to autograph my cast? See, there's still a little space left."

"Hey, yeah." The puzzled look left William's face as he turned his attention to my cast. "Who else signed it? Did Scott sign it?"

William liked Scott, probably because Scott treated him like a person, not just a know-nothing little kid.

"Scott signed it right here." I pointed to his name and the phone number of his hospital room.

"Let's see who else is on there." William twisted his head to peer at the names.

As if the show was over, Mom and Dad moved from their places in the audience.

Mom touched Dad's arm. "Will you take Ja-nine's suitcase upstairs, Don? I'll go fix some lunch. Guess what we're having, Janine."

"Enchiladas," William tattled. "I'd rather have hamburgers."

Mom tweaked his nose as she passed him.

"We'll have hamburgers when it's a special day for you. This is Janine Day, and she likes enchiladas." She headed for the kitchen.

Dad picked up my suitcase. "Why don't you take Janine to a chair, William? You can read her arm better when she's sitting down." He went on upstairs.

William took my good arm and guided me to a chair into which I sank gratefully. I was feeling woozy. William fell to his knees beside me so he could go on examining the signatures on my cast.

"There's Catherine," he said, proud that he could recognize her name. "Who's this?" He pointed at another name.

"Hallie," I said. "My roommate at the hospital. Hallie Markovitch. She was in an accident, too." I thought about Hallie and what the nurse's aide had said about her. I was sure she'd be all right. When her boyfriend, Kevin, came home and visited her, she would want to get better.

I pointed to another name. "Here's Rafe Belmont. He's Scott's roommate at the hospital."

"Wow," William breathed. "You mean the real Rafe Belmont who makes all the touchdowns at the football games?"

"That's the one."

"Wow." William touched the name reverently.

"There's a place right next to his name where I could sign. Okay?"

I nodded, and William got a felt-tip pen from Mom's desk. He wrote W-I-L-L-I-A-M P-A-L-M-E-R in big, scrawly letters.

"There, how's that?" he asked.

"Terrific." I ruffled his hair. I needed to talk to him before Mom and Dad came back. It was hard to know where to start. "William," I said. "What did you mean before when you asked if I was really Janine?"

He glanced at me, then his eyes went back to my cast. "You just seemed different. That's all."

I put my hand under his chin and turned his head so he looked at me again. "In what way did I seem different?"

His eyes slid away and he shrugged. "Oh, you know. I never saw you with that white thing on your head and your arm in a cast and all."

An empty feeling started somewhere in my mid-section and spread throughout my body. Had it really just been my outward appearance William had noticed? Was I alone again with my secret?

"Are you sure that's all, William?"

He removed his chin from my hand and rolled away from me on the floor. "Sure it is. Hey, did you know that David moved away while you were gone? My friend David? He said he was going to but I didn't really believe he would." William got to his knees and crawled toward me. "I went to his house and knocked on the door and some strange guy answered it. David's not there anymore."

There was pain in William's eyes, and I felt it reflected in my own. Was that what was going to happen to me? If I didn't do something about my problem, would somebody knock someday soon and Lenore would answer the door?

The special lunch Mom fixed was delicious. I tucked away three of the enchiladas, enjoying every bite.

Lenore enjoyed them, too.

"That hospital food was nowhere," she said in the midst of my third enchilada. *"I didn't know anything could be as good as this. Are we having something else, too?"*

We were. Apple pie and ice cream. Lenore almost freaked out. She said she could remember the taste of ice cream, but the other things were all new to her.

I groaned after I'd eaten a big piece of pie. "It's good we don't have Janine Day every week or I'd weigh a ton."

"This is a once-in-a-lifetime day." Mom smiled. "Have another piece."

"*Oh, please,*" Lenore pleaded.

I was feeling great, there with the family that I loved, and I couldn't help but have sympathy for Lenore who'd been part of it for such a short time.

So I had a second piece for her.

When I finally went up to my room, escorted by Mom and Dad with William tagging along, I found that a telephone extension had been installed by the side of my bed.

"So you can reach out and touch someone whenever you want," Dad said.

He and Mom fussed over me, getting me installed in my familiar bed for a nap, while William peeked around the door frame without coming into my room.

Mom pulled down the window shades. "There's a buzzer on the phone. Just give it a punch if you need anything and one of us will come running."

"Poop," William complained. "How come I can't have a buzzer?"

"Because you've never been sick or hurt bad," Mom said. "And don't say *poop.*"

"I had my tonsils out," he said. "I didn't get any buzzer then. Poop."

Mom put an arm around his shoulders. "You

wouldn't stay in bed, either, remember? And you got to eat ice cream all day long for three days." She turned to me. "Have a good nap, Janine. Push the buzzer if you want us to come."

"All the comforts of the hospital!" I was embarrassed by the attention. They were treating me like a little kid. "I can get around now, Mom. If I need something, I can get it."

Mom came over to give me a hug. "Let us spoil you a little. We're just so glad to have you back that I guess we want to do everything for you."

Dad came over to pat my arm awkwardly, then they all tiptoed out, leaving me alone in the cool darkness.

No, not alone.

"I'd forgotten what it's like," Lenore said when they were gone.

"What do you mean?" I was ready for sleep and I lay there quietly, only my eyes moving, checking out the familiar objects in my room. It hadn't changed. The twin beds were there—mine and the one reserved for guests who stayed over. The one that would have been Lenore's if she'd lived.

Then there were my bookshelves. My dresser, cluttered with bottles of hand lotion and jars of face cream I'd hoped would fade my freckles and the mole under my chin. The red-and-white pennant from my high school. My big poster of some mythical place with a spired castle rising out of the mists and peaked mountains in the background.

Were those the tall crystal mountains I'd seen when I was whirring around somewhere in space?

Lenore was still speaking. *"I'd forgotten what it's like to be part of a family. It makes you feel all warm and safe. And loved."*

"You got it," I said drowsily.

My eyes continued their travels over the blue-flowered wallpaper and the white tieback curtains. To my desk that stood between the two windows. To the photo that stood there. Mom and Dad and William and me.

Our family.

Lenore's family. She was part of it. Part of us. She deserved to be there with us.

But not this way. Not with me, in *my* body.

Not sharing *my* life.

Couldn't she see there was really no longer a place for her? In the picture we were arranged in a formal pose with Mom and Dad sitting side by side and William standing between them with me right behind him. Artistic. Complete. If Lenore had been there it would have been totally rearranged, a different picture entirely.

The ringing of the telephone broke off my thoughts and brought me out of the soft comfort of sleep. I lifted the receiver.

"Janine?" It was Scott. I was glad he called.

"Hullo? Hullo?" Evidently William had picked up the phone downstairs. "Who's this?" he demanded.

"It's for me, William," I said firmly.

"Who is it?"

Scott chuckled. "Hiya, buddy. It's me. Scott."

"Hi, Scott," William said. "Is Rafe there, too?"

"Sure, he's here." Scott sounded puzzled.

"Can I talk to him?" William asked.

"William," I broke in. "You can talk to Rafe on your own time. Scott called to talk to *me*."

"Poop," William complained. "How come everything's always for you?"

"William, I haven't seen Boomer since I got home," I said. "Why don't you go find him and bring him up to see me?"

"Well, okay." William sounded reluctant. "Dumb dog's probably over at Anna Mae's." He hung up.

"His nose is out of joint," I explained to Scott. "This has been Janine Day here."

"It's been Janine Day here, too," Scott said. "I've been thinking about you ever since you left."

"Did you and Rafe finish your chess game?" Why was *I* talking about Rafe?

"Sure. He won again. I'm no match for that guy." He gave a little laugh. "It's like living with a movie star, having him around. I can't count all the girls who've been here to visit him."

I felt a twinge of jealousy. It had to have come from Lenore.

"Don't even try to count them." I didn't want to hear about all those girls.

We talked about hospital food and school and the weather and all those safe things. We didn't mention Scott's impending operation.

I could hear background noises and laughter. Were some of those girls visiting Rafe right now?

What did I care?

After Scott said good-bye, I drifted off to sleep and dreamed that I was out under the tree in front of our house and Scott came running toward me, his legs healed and good again. In the dream he grabbed me up and kissed me and I felt all warm and safe and wanted to stay there close to him.

"Oh, Scott," I said.

But when I looked again, it was Rafe who held me.

Lenore woke me up. She was disturbed, and I was aware that my eyes were already open.

Had she opened them?

William stood there in the dim room, holding Boomer by the collar. I reached out and switched on a lamp so I could see Boomer's dear old dog face.

Lenore reacted with alarm.

"Get that beast out of here," I heard my voice say in slurred but understandable words, and I had another of those memory flashes. My twin had hated dogs. She'd cried whenever one came near her.

Boomer, sweet, smelly old dog, stiffened and his upper lip raised to show his fangs. He growled, deep in his throat.

"*Lenore,*" I cried. "*I won't let you do this. You can't take over my voice.*"

"It's all right," I said, reaching my hand out to the dog. "I'm sorry, Boomer. Here, boy. Come here to me."

Boomer hesitated a moment, then relaxed. His tail wagged and he bounded over to greet me.

William watched with wide, knowing eyes. If he hadn't known before that there was something strange about me, he did now.

SEVEN

This time I wasn't going to make the mistake of questioning William. It just made him evasive. It was enough to know for sure that he'd sensed something different about me. I would use that knowledge later, when the time was right.

"William," I said, "would you like me to watch some of your videotapes with you?"

He seemed pleased. "How about Wallace and Gromit?"

I nodded. "Sure. Anything you'd like."

William smiled happily. "Anna Mae doesn't like Wallace and Gromit. I don't get to watch them anymore."

Poor William, henpecked already. "Where *is* Anna Mae?" I asked. She generally spent most of her life at our house.

"She's visiting her grandma." There was relief in William's voice.

While he went to get the video, I tried to make friends with Boomer again. He'd been sitting by the door watching me suspiciously. But since Lenore didn't try any more funny stuff, he finally came over and let me scratch behind his ears.

Good old Boomer. He might be helpful, too, when it came time to prove to Mom and Dad that Lenore was there with me.

By the time we'd finished the video and William had gone off to do something else, Dad was home.

He came upstairs and hovered over me, asking if he could bring me something, anything. He sat on my bed and patted my shoulder awkwardly.

I liked having him there. It reminded me of when I was a child. When I was his "good little Janny." I liked being good. I was rewarded for being good. When I was bad, it was Lenore's fault.

"Dad," I said. "Do you ever think much about Lenore?"

"Lenore? You asked about her not that long ago. Have you been thinking about her?"

I shrugged. "I guess. I have a lot of time to think about a lot of things right now. *Do* you ever think about her?"

Dad looked out my window, off into the distance. "It was a long time ago that we lost her. I've been so involved with my work and everything. I guess I have to say I don't really think a whole lot about her much anymore. Only now and then."

"How do you like that, Lenore?" I said. *"Dad barely remembers you. He doesn't want you back."*

"You're cruel," Lenore whispered. *"You didn't have to do that."*

I wasn't normally cruel. But it wasn't normal having Lenore pushing into my space, either. She brought out the worst in me.

"Mind if I stay here and talk till dinner's ready?" Dad asked. "Mom said if you needed me she'd let me off KP duty."

"Love to have you." I snuggled against his arm, warm and secure in the knowledge that he didn't think about Lenore much anymore.

The next morning Dad went to work and William went to school full of importance because he could tell about how his sister had Rafe Belmont's autograph on her arm cast.

I felt a lot better that day, well enough to walk around and explore the house. I wandered into Mom's studio where she was just starting a new painting. She's an artist and spends a lot of time there in her studio.

"I didn't know you were up," she said when she saw me. "What can I get for you?"

I put a hand up to tell her to stay where she was. "I'm just touring," I said. "It's so good to be home."

"There's no place like home, as they say," Mom said.

"*Ask her,*" Lenore whispered.

"*Ask her what?*"

"*Ask her the same thing that you asked Dad. Ask her if she ever thinks about me.*"

"*Her answer will be the same as Dad's, Lenore.*"

"*Are you afraid to ask? Do you think she'll love you any less if she remembers me? Ask her.*"

I could feel Lenore's anxiety.

I walked over to Mom's canvas and touched its edge. "What are you painting this time, Mom?"

"Oh . . ." The word came out almost as a sigh.

"I've been feeling a little nostalgic lately." She waved her brush at a photograph of our house that she'd tacked to the wall. "I'm doing a painting of the house the way it was before we remodeled and added to it. The way it was when your father and I first bought it."

I squinted at the photo. Our house looked squatty and sawed off without the addition of the garage and William's room over it. That's the way it must have looked when I was born. When Lenore and I were born.

"Mom, do you ever think about Lenore?"

Mom looked surprised, but then she smiled and said, "Funny you should ask about her. I've been thinking about her a lot lately. About losing her. Maybe because we so recently almost lost you, too." She made a couple of brush strokes on her canvas. "Yes, I still think about Lenore a lot. A mother never forgets her babies."

"She was the naughty one," I reminded Mom.

Mom glanced at me. "She *was* naughty sometimes, but she was a darling little girl. I loved her so much."

"*I told you so,*" Lenore chortled. "*Mom would never forget me.*"

"*That doesn't mean she wants you back, Lenore.*"

But my harsh words didn't diminish Lenore's happiness, which was so strong that I felt uplifted myself.

"Speaking of Lenore," Mom said, "I wonder if I can find a painting I did several years ago." She walked over to a closet where she keeps her old paintings and began rummaging around.

The doorbell rang. "I'll answer it," I said. "You keep looking."

"Okay," Mom's voice was muffled in the closet, "if you're up to dispatching a pushy salesman."

"I'll whack him with my arm cast." I headed down the hallway to the living room and front door.

I wasn't prepared to see Rafe Belmont on the steps when I opened the door.

"Hi," he said cheerfully. "I got my pardon from the hospital today so I thought I'd drop around and see you."

He was leaning on crutches. His wicked dark eyes sparkled in the sunlight, making goose bumps rise on my arms.

It was I who asked Rafe how Scott was doing, but it was Lenore who motioned for him to come into the house. Then it was I who didn't know what to say to him since Lenore couldn't speak well enough yet to be understood.

I cleared my throat. "You must be feeling pretty good if you're tooling around alone already."

"No sweat," Rafe said. "I won't be playing football for a while, but I can get around just fine with the help of my wooden legs here." He held up one of the crutches.

There was a moment of silence while I figured out what to say next. I cleared my throat again, blushing. I couldn't believe *Rafe Belmont* was right there in my living room.

"Won't you sit down?" I asked finally.

"No." Rafe shook his head. "I just dropped by to ask if you'd go out with me."

I was so surprised I couldn't say anything.

But Lenore could.

"Yes," she said. She slurred the word a little, but it was clear enough.

"Yes what? Yes, you'll go out with me?"

"Yes," Lenore repeated.

"Hey, great." Rafe sounded pleased and a little surprised. His dark eyes snapped with vitality. I was frightened by him—and excited.

"I mean," he continued, "I don't want to be cutting Scott out while he's still in the hospital, but then again I knew a girl like you wouldn't want to sit around reading the autographs on her cast."

Lenore stretched my mouth into a smile. "That's right."

It came out more like "Thash right," and Rafe looked at me quizzically. But all he said was, "Will you be well enough to go out on Friday night?"

"Yes," Lenore said.

"Great. I'll pick you up about seven o'clock. We'll see what we're both up to doing then. Okay?"

"Okay," Lenore agreed.

Why didn't I protest? I was stronger than Lenore. But I didn't say anything.

I had jumbled thoughts of Scott as I walked Rafe to the door. What would he say about my going out with Rafe?

Did he have to know?

Lenore said good-bye to Rafe, then to me she said, *"I can't believe it. Rafe came to see* me."

Of course. He was *Lenore's* date, not mine. *I* couldn't possibly go out with him since I was Scott's girl, but Lenore could, couldn't she? Just once. Just while Scott was still in the hospital. It was all right.

"Janine," Mom called. "Janine, come back in here and see what I've found." Her voice was about three steps up the scale from its normal pitch, which meant she was excited about something.

I hurried back to her studio as fast as my rubbery legs would go. She was standing there by her easel, holding a medium-size canvas up to the light to see it better.

She thrust the canvas toward me. I looked at it and saw two little faces looking back at me. Two little girl faces.

"I did this painting of you and Lenore years ago," Mom said. "I'd almost forgotten it." A memory, or some fragment of a memory, ricocheted through me. It was something about the painting, or at least something that had to do with the painting.

I tried to close my eyes to keep Lenore from seeing those two little faces, but she fought back, pulling my eyelids up and focusing my eyes on the painting.

"I want to see that, Janine," she cried. *"That's a painting of both of us. Why won't you let me look at it?"*

"No." I struggled to look at Mom, at the far corners of the room, anywhere but at the painting. Seeing the painting would only strengthen Lenore's opinion that she belonged there in our home.

But more than that, I feared the memory that was trying to claw its way back into my consciousness.

"Look at it," Lenore cried. *"We shared space before we were born. We'll share space on that canvas until it crumbles. Why can't you share space with me now?"*

I stared at the painting, letting her take a good look at it. *"It must be obvious even to you, Lenore, that there are two babies there. Two bodies. We were never meant to share one body."*

I tried to close my eyes again, tried to look anywhere but at the painting. But Lenore fought me. I must have looked freaky with my eyelids fluttering and my eyes rolling all around because Mom dropped the painting and grabbed my arm.

"Janine!" She helped me to a chair. "Oh, how stupid of me. Here, honey, sit down."

I sat.

"I'm okay, Mom," I said shakily. "I guess I just hurried in here too fast."

Mom fanned my face with a small canvas she snatched from her worktable. "I shouldn't have shoved that painting at you that way."

"That's not it, Mom. It was the hurrying. Truly." I stood up. "I'd like to see the painting again now, please."

Mom shoved me back down onto the chair. "I'll get it. Are you sure you can handle it now?"

"Sure. It's just that I didn't even know that painting existed."

She picked the canvas up off the floor. "I did it a few years after Lenore died, but then I couldn't bear to look at it so I put it away. I guess I never did show it to you."

Which of course was why I had no memory of it. But there was something that I'd almost remembered when I saw the painting.

It was as if a flashbulb had gone off in my memory, but what it illuminated was gone before I could examine it. Still, I knew what it was. A photograph of two little girls, turned slightly to face one another, like mirror images. "Didn't you used to have a photo of Lenore and me? Almost like the painting?"

"Yes." Mom gazed at the canvas. "I did the painting from that photo, just the way I'm doing the painting of our house now. The picture was taken when we were all up in Idaho, a few days before . . ." She stopped, and her face was sad.

"I remember that photo." I knew something about it—but I hadn't known I knew until that memory flash, triggered by the painting. "Where is it now?"

Mom shook her head. "I don't know. It's been missing for years. Probably buried in a box somewhere."

I took the painting from Mom's hands and let my eyes linger on both of the small faces.

Mom is good at doing faces, and she'd caught the incomplete, unfinished look that small children have.

"Mom," I said, "tell me about the day Lenore died."

Mom sighed. "It's not a thing I like to talk about."

"Please."

Mom looked at the painting. The two little girls wore T-shirts, one blue and one pink, with names embroidered on the fronts. The child on the left with the blue shirt was Lenore and the one on the right in the pink was me.

"You were so much alike," Mom said softly. "It was hard to tell you apart, even for us. We always put your names on your clothes to make it easier to tell who was who. Your grandmother made those little shirts you were wearing on the day of the picture, and on the day . . ." She stopped again.

She put her head down for a moment, then raised it, brushing at her eyes. "It was when we were visiting Grandma and Grandpa Palmer in Idaho that Lenore died. Grandma and I were busy canning peaches, and your dad and Grandpa were off doing something in the fields. I guess no one was watching you girls. You wandered off to the barnyard, to the duck pond."

"Lenore said we should go there," I said. Did I remember that?

Mom smiled. "Lenore was always the adventuresome one."

"See?" I said to Lenore. *"It wasn't my fault af-ter all. It was yours."*

"Think about it," she said. *"Remember it."*

"Somehow you both got into the pond," Mom said. "You got out, but Lenore . . ." Mom hunched over, her voice shaking.

I put a hand on her shoulder. "I know, Mom. I ran up to the house to tell you to come."

How did I know that? Had somebody told me or was I remembering that, too?

Mom raised her head, scrubbing a hand across her face. "Yes. But when we got to the pond, it was too late."

But how could it have been my fault? I was only four years old.

Lenore's claim was ridiculous. But how could I prove it? Nobody else had been there when we went into the water.

Was that another memory?

I shivered. I didn't want to remember anymore.

"May I take the painting up to my room?" I asked. "I'd like to look at it some more."

"Sure." Mom gazed at the faces of the two little girls. "I loved her so much."

"I know." I took the painting.

"Why can't we tell her I'm here?" Lenore said

as I climbed the stairs. *"You just heard her say how much she loves me."*

"Loved, Lenore. Past tense. It would freak her out to know you're here now. It's just too . . . too . . ." I searched for the right word. *"It's just too grotesque."*

The ugly word silenced her. She subsided, and I felt her sadness. By the time I got to my room, I could feel my chest heaving. Tears flowed from my eyes.

Lenore was crying.

For just a little while, I cried with her.

EIGHT

I couldn't help but feel sorry for Lenore, so I agreed to grant her a few days during which I wouldn't constantly poke and jab at her. I wouldn't try to make her leave. I would give her those few days to let her experience the world with me.

She was my sister.

In return Lenore agreed she would stop trying to control my body. She would go along with whatever I wanted to do, on one condition: I would allow her to keep her date with Rafe on Friday. To tell the truth, I wasn't too hard to convince.

The week bumped along with Mom and Dad leaping up to get whatever I wanted, whenever I wanted it. It made me nervous, but I knew it was just their great relief over not losing a second daughter that made them act that way.

Sometimes I wished they would talk about the accident. I wished they would demand to know what Scott and I were doing at that intersection when we were supposed to be in school. I wished they would yell at me for breaking the rules.

I wished they would blame Scott for the whole thing. I didn't have a clue as to why they didn't blame him, why they weren't on his case for almost killing me.

On Thursday, I had an appointment with Dr. Zeigler to have some of my bandages removed. I planned to visit Hallie and Scott while I was at the hospital. I hadn't heard from Scott since his operation. I figured he would call when he was able. I told myself that was why I didn't call him.

The truth was I felt guilty about talking with him when I was planning to go out with Rafe. It was Lenore's date, of course, I kept assuring myself, but she couldn't go without me.

Mom drove me to the hospital. I told her to come back in about an hour since she had some shopping to do.

"Are you sure you'll be all right?" she asked. "You're still a little shaky, you know."

I wondered how long it would be before she stopped hovering. "If I feel faint, Mom, what better place could I be than in a hospital?"

Mom laughed. "Good point. See you in an hour."

I almost wished she'd stayed with me when the familiar hospital odors surrounded me. Memories flooded back. Not pleasant memories like when I smell lavender and remember my grandmother's spotless little house in Idaho. My hospital memories were made up of pain and despair and even horror. I had to will my legs to carry me along the corridor to Dr. Zeigler's office.

My visit with her was short. She examined me, removed some bandages, and said I was doing fine but shouldn't try to go to school for the rest of the term, which was only a few weeks.

That was all right with me. Catherine kept me up to date on all the campus happenings, and my teachers sent assignments home. I didn't really feel like sitting through classes. Especially not with unpredictable Lenore sitting there with me.

After I finished with Dr. Zeigler, I went to visit Hallie. I went to her room before going to see Scott because then I wouldn't have to cut my time with him short.

Or was it because I wanted to take up as much

time as I could with Hallie so I wouldn't have to stay as long with Scott?

What was the matter with me? Why should I feel guilty about Lenore's date with Rafe? Scott didn't own me.

The bed that had been mine was empty, and Hallie was asleep when I got to the room I'd shared with her. She looked small and caved in under the white sheet. I'd hoped to find her looking healthy and robust, ready to go out soon for those burgers we'd promised ourselves. But it was obvious it wouldn't be in the near future. Maybe the motor-mouth nurse's aide had been right.

Hallie had apparently dropped off to sleep in the midst of writing a letter, because her metal table was still positioned across her bed and her right arm rested on it, a pen clutched between her fingers. There was a box of stationery on one corner of the table, and I was easing a sheet of paper out of it when Hallie woke up. She seemed startled.

"I was just going to write you a note," I explained.

"Oh, it's you, Janine." She put a hand to her chest. "I wasn't expecting to see you. I was dreaming about somebody else."

"Kevin," I said.

I thought that would make her smile, but it didn't. I blabbered on. "I mean, who else would be playing the leading man in your dreams?"

Hallie slowly shook her head. "There isn't any leading man in *my* dreams."

I had never seen her depressed like that. Usually a few corny cracks would have her grinning around those wires.

"Well," I pursued relentlessly. "Kevin will apply for the job as soon as he comes."

"He's not coming," she said shortly.

"You mean he's still in Hawaii? I thought he was coming home soon."

"He's home," she said evenly. "Has been for a while. My mother saw him." She closed her eyes. "He hasn't even called me."

"But why?" I bleated before I could stop myself from making things worse. "You're his girl."

Tears ran out of Hallie's squeezed-shut eyes and red blotches colored her cheeks.

Oh, boy. I'd really blundered.

I took her hand. "I'm sorry. I shouldn't have come. All I've done is make you miserable."

Hallie shook her head and scrubbed at her eyes. "I was miserable long before you came." She took a deep, shaky breath, sniffing back the tears, then opened her reddened eyes. "I'm not very good company today, am I? The least I could do is ask how it is out in the big, bright world."

I thought about her question. "It's not the same as it was," I said finally.

She showed a spark of interest. "How do you mean?"

"I don't know exactly. I guess after a bad accident you realize how fragile you are. It changes your outlook."

Hallie nodded slowly. "But you're not one of the fragile ones, Janine. There's a lot more to you than there is to most of us. You're a survivor."

Something pinged again in that part of my mind that had been giving me flashes of memory. Something to do with surviving, but like the other flashes it was gone before I could examine it.

"You're a survivor, too, Hallie," I told her. "Everything will turn out all right. You'll see."

My words sounded stupid, but for the first time Hallie smiled. "Yes," she said. "We'll see."

Lenore was upset at Kevin when we left Hallie's room.

"*What's the matter with that creep?*" she asked.

"*Doesn't he know that the thought of him is what kept her going?*"

I was surprised at Lenore's perception. But then I guess she knew all about rejection.

"*People can't always be counted on,*" I said, as the elevator door opened and I got on, pushing the button for Scott's floor.

"*But,*" she objected, "*why can't he wait until she's well before he drops her? Why does he have to break her heart when everything else is broken?*"

"Broken hearts are part of the Great Experience, Lenore," I said. "It's a package deal. You have to take the bad along with the good. Hallie knows that."

"*She's not strong enough,*" Lenore said. "*Can't you see she's not strong enough?*"

I didn't answer, and Lenore changed the subject.

"*Why didn't you go to see Scott first?*" She paused. "*You don't want to see him, do you?*"

So what was she doing now, invading my mind as well as my body? Abruptly I lost any good feelings I had toward her.

"You *wouldn't* understand, Lenore," I muttered.

"*You haven't been to see him since you left here,*" Lenore nagged. "*You're as bad as Kevin.*"

This was a real role reversal, Lenore feeling compassion.

"Drop it, Lenore. I don't want to hear your opinions." The elevator stopped and the doors opened. I quickened my steps as I hurried down the corridor toward Scott's room.

But the room was empty. Both beds were stripped and doubled over, as if neither former occupant was expected back.

My heart thumped as I headed for the nearest nurse's station.

Why hadn't I called Scott yesterday, or the day before? Why hadn't he called me? Surely I would have heard if something had happened to him. His parents would have called me. Wouldn't they? Or didn't they want him to associate with me? Did they think I had led him into cutting school that day and piling up at the intersection?

A nurse was filing patient charts at the desk, her head bent low over her work. Her hair was dark with an inch of gray showing at the roots.

"Uh," I said, hoping she would look up. "Uh, Miss?" Maybe that title didn't show proper respect for those gray roots. "Ma'am?" I tried. My throat was so dry my voice sounded raspy.

Still she didn't look up. I glanced down the long

corridor to see if there was another nurse in sight. All I could see was a young male nurse taking an elderly man for a stroll with one of those metal walker things that old people use.

"Nurse?"

I had one of those crazy feelings you get sometimes when nobody will pay attention to you and you have a flash of fright that some Twilight Zone thing has happened and you have become invisible. I wondered if that was how Lenore felt. Maybe we had changed places. Maybe she was now the owner of the body and I just existed inside her head, silent and lost.

In sudden terror I reached out and touched the nurse on the shoulder. She jumped and looked up at me with startled eyes.

"Oh, my stars, you gave me a turn," she said. "Were you talking to me, dear?"

I nodded dumbly, too relieved to speak.

She stood up. "Sorry. Guess I had my hearing aid turned too low."

I thought she was kidding like people do when they don't hear what you've said, but she reached up and adjusted something at her ear. "Now, what can I do for you?" she asked, eyeing my arm cast. "Are you a patient or a visitor?" She wrinkled her forehead, apparently trying to remember if I belonged on her floor.

"I'm looking for Scott Nelson," I said. "His room is empty."

The nurse nodded. "Oh, yes. Scott. He's still up in ICU."

"ICU?" I tried to remember hospital terminology.

"Intensive Care Unit," the nurse said. "He had a bit of trouble after the operation."

My mouth became a desert. I had to choke my words out. "What happened? Is he all right?"

"He's doing as well as can be expected," the nurse said.

As well as can be expected—that could mean anything.

"May I see him? Just for a minute?"

"Are you family, dear?"

I shook my head.

"The best thing for you to do then is to call the nurse who's taking care of him. Here, I'll give you the unit phone number." She scribbled on a slip of paper and handed it to me. "I'm afraid you can't see him, dear."

"Thanks." Clutching the paper, I fled back to the elevator. Past all the rooms with people filed away in them. Where was Scott filed? Was he all right?

"I'm sorry about Scott," Lenore said.

Maybe she was. I wondered how much sorrier she'd be when I told her that she wouldn't be going out with Rafe the next night. How could I go traipsing around on a date when Scott might be dangerously ill?

Now wasn't the time to tell her since I had no idea how she'd react. I didn't want her doing anything in the hospital that would make them keep me here.

Mom wasn't at the front entrance when I got there, so I went into the gift shop. Anything to get my mind off Scott. Maybe I should call the number the nurse had given me. But could I handle what she might tell me?

The only person in the gift shop was a saleswoman in a gray volunteer's smock. I couldn't imagine volunteering to be in a hospital, even in a gift shop. Maybe it was a lot different when you had a choice.

The saleswoman smiled at me as I entered. "May I help you, dear?"

Did hospital personnel go through some sort of training course where they learned to call everybody "dear"?

"I'm just looking, thank you," I said.

She nodded. "If you see anything you like, let me know."

That wasn't likely. I didn't want any magazines, paperback books, or fuzzy stuffed animals. I fingered some of the gold chains that dangled from a rack and poked at a tray of enameled bracelets and rings, just to have something to do.

Then I saw the flowered blue enamel bracelet. It was exactly my favorite shade of blue. It would look terrific with the blue-striped blouse I'd been planning to wear for Lenore's date with Rafe.

How could I even think of that now? *"Lenore,"* I said, thinking I would tell her right now that the date was off, no matter what the consequences.

But she interrupted. *"I like that,"* she said, and I found myself trying the bracelet on my undamaged arm.

Surely it wouldn't hurt to see how it looked.

"Blue is my favorite color," Lenore said.

108   I had another of those memory flashes. I remembered that Lenore's shirt in the lost photograph was blue.

"Let's get it," she said. *"You can wear it for my date with Rafe."*

"Lenore," I said again, then stopped. I looked

at the price tag. *"Seventy-nine ninety-five."* I shucked the bracelet off my arm and put it back in the display tray. *"It's too expensive."*

"Oh, please get it for me," Lenore wheedled. *"I've never owned anything like that. I love it."*

She sounded like a ten-year-old, begging for a toy. Maybe she had to go through all the stages she'd missed.

But it was impossible.

"I don't have enough money." I opened my purse and looked inside my wallet where two dollar bills and a couple of quarters lived.

"Oh, please, please, please. I'll never ask for anything else. Just the bracelet. I need it."

"Forget it," I said. I put the wallet back inside my purse.

Before I even had a chance to close my purse, I felt my arm moving. Startled, I watched it reach out, pick up the blue bracelet, and drop it inside the purse.

"LENORE," I yelled. I tried to take the bracelet out of my purse, but Lenore resisted. The saleswoman looked over at me curiously. "Find something you like, dear?"

What could I do? I couldn't fish the bracelet out while she was watching. How could I ever explain to her that Lenore was the one who'd taken it?

The saleswoman kept looking my way. I smiled at her.

"Just looking," I said and walked out of the store with the bracelet nestled there deep inside my purse.

NINE

Mom drove up just as I hurried out of the gift shop. I got into the car, the secret in my purse so hot that it could have been burning a hole.

"Hi," Mom said. "How is Scott?"

"Not good. He had some trouble after the operation."

I didn't tell her I hadn't even seen him. Maybe it was because I didn't want her to ask where I'd been since she'd left.

"I'm sorry to hear he's having problems," Mom said.

She went on chatting about people she knew who'd had serious operations and had lived to tell about it.

I hardly listened. My mind was on the bracelet.

"Lenore," I said inside my head. *"You can't do that. Stealing is wrong."*

She didn't answer. Like a guilty child, she was hiding.

"Just wait till we get home," I threatened.

But when we did get home, I wasn't sure what I could do to punish Lenore.

Mom fixed a snack, but I couldn't eat much.

"Aren't you feeling well, honey?" Mom put her palm against my forehead the way she'd done when I was a little kid and had a fever.

"I'm all right, Mom. I'm just worried about Scott."

"He's a very strong young man, Janine. He'll be all right." She gave me a reassuring smile. "Go upstairs now and try to get some rest. I'm worried about you."

I took her suggestion and went upstairs, closing my bedroom door. Out of guilt? I didn't usually close it.

Putting my purse with its stolen burden on my bed, I fished around in it with my good hand until I found the bracelet.

"Lenore, we have something to discuss." I spoke aloud. It seemed more forceful that way, and I needed all the force I could muster. How do you confront someone who is only a voice inside your head? I couldn't fix Lenore with a fiery eye and make her *see* how outraged I was.

Or could I?

Walking over to my dresser, I faced the mirror. Looking myself straight in the eye, I called Lenore again, louder than before.

"*I can hear you,*" Lenore said. "*Very likely Mom can hear you and maybe even Hallie over at the hospital, too. What are you yelling about?*"

I stared at my own face, which was bunched together with anger. The brows hung low over the eyes and the mouth was a straight slash across the lower part of my face. Even Lenore should be able to see how angry I was.

I held up the bracelet I'd taken from my purse. "This is what I'm yelling about, Lenore."

"*Oh, the bracelet!*" Lenore said it with delight, as if I'd brought the bracelet out of my purse purely for her pleasure. "*Put it on your arm so I can see how it looks.*"

"Are you crazy? It's stolen. It's not mine."

"*Of course it isn't yours. It's mine. Now put it on.*"

"Lenore!"

"*Here, I'll do it.*"

I watched as Lenore took the bracelet in the hand of my broken arm, squeezing together the fingers of my left hand and deftly slipping the bracelet onto my arm.

"Lenore!" I gasped. "You promised not to use my arms anymore."

"*Well, you wouldn't put on the bracelet,*" she said defensively. "*What was I supposed to do?*"

There was no way to reason with her. She was a child. A naughty child.

I sighed. "Lenore. The bracelet is not yours. You stole it. We have to take it back to the gift shop."

"*So okay. We'll take it back. When's the next time we'll be going to the hospital?*"

"I don't know. I'll get Mom to drive me back there today."

"*Look.*" Lenore spoke patiently. "*We'll get Rafe to take us to the hospital to see Scott tomorrow night. We can return the bracelet then. In the meantime, we can enjoy it.*"

It was tempting.

Then I remembered. "You're not going out with Rafe tomorrow night, Lenore. I can't go out with somebody else when Scott is so sick."

"*Rafe's my date, sister dear. I'll never get another chance to go out with a guy. When Scott gets out of the hospital, we'll go out only with him, of*

course. But until then? What's it going to hurt?"
She sounded as if she might cry again.

So maybe she was right. Maybe I needed a night out.

Tomorrow was soon enough to return the bracelet. Very likely the volunteer at the gift shop hadn't even noticed it was missing. If she had, she probably figured one of the other volunteers had sold it.

"See how pretty it looks." Lenore turned my arm in front of my eyes.

I sputtered a little, but I couldn't deny that what Lenore said was true. The bracelet felt smooth and cool against the skin of my arm, and it looked as if it belonged there.

It wasn't as if I'd get it dirty or damage it by wearing it for a little while.

"Okay, Lenore, we'll take it back tomorrow night. But I don't want you taking any more things that don't belong to you. Do you understand?"

"I won't do it again. But don't you just love it?"

That was when I heard the low growl behind me. Lenore was still speaking when I noticed in the mirror that my bedroom door was partly open. William and Anna Mae stood there, staring at me with enormous eyes. William had hold of Boomer's collar and it was Boomer who was growling. It was like he'd done the day I came home.

"See?" William whispered to Anna Mae. "It was worth it, wasn't it?"

Anna Mae nodded solemnly, her eyes glinting behind her thick glasses. "He charged me fifty cents to see you," she told me.

How long had they been there? How much had they heard? Why had I taken the chance of speaking aloud to Lenore?

Even worse, had Lenore been using my voice to speak aloud? I wasn't sure.

"Oh, hi there, kids." I sounded phony and dumb. "I'm rehearsing a part for a play I'm trying out for. I'm doing it in front of my mirror so I can get my gestures right."

"What play?" Anna Mae asked.

"A play at school."

Anna Mae eyed me, unblinking as a snake. "What's the name of the play?"

I searched my memory for the title of a play. Any play.

"It's called *Romeo and Juliet,*" I said. That was safe. What would an eight-year-old kid know about *Romeo and Juliet*?

"I saw it on TV," Anna Mae stated.

I was afraid she was going to ask me to quote lines, but all she said was "When's it going to be?"

Why couldn't Miss Wise Eyes Anna Mae just accept what I said and shut up? Why was she poking around in my lies like somebody looking for a diamond ring in a bag of worms? Pretty soon she'd be asking for tickets.

I managed a silly little laugh. "I probably won't even get a part. I'm not very good at acting."

"That's true," Anna Mae said.

Taking William's hand, she yanked him along with her down the stairs, leaving Boomer staring at me, his tail wagging tentatively.

I didn't tell Mom and Dad about the date with Rafe until just before dinner the next night.

"Rafe's coming by to pick me up in a little while," I said as we were sitting down at the table. "We're going to go to the hospital to see Scott."

"Rafe?" Mom asked. "Do I know a Rafe?"

"I think I've mentioned him," I lied. "He was Scott's roommate at the hospital."

"Mom," William said, "don't you know about Rafe Belmont? He's the one who makes all the touchdowns in the high-school football games."

"He just had a knee operation," I explained.

"We're going to go see Scott," I added in case Mom and Dad had missed it the first time.

"I've read about him in the sports section," Dad said, taking some mashed potatoes and passing the bowl around.

"Oh." Mom's face smoothed out. "When did you talk to him, Janine?"

"He called this afternoon."

The lies came so easily now. But Catherine had called, so I knew Mom had heard the phone ring. There was no way she could know it hadn't been Rafe.

"Is Rafe going to be in the play, too?" William asked.

I shook my head, then to change the subject said, "William, don't be so gross with your food."

I hoped that would divert William's attention from the nonexistent play. It was appropriate at any meal to tell him not to mess with his food. Tonight he was building a canal with his mashed potatoes so his gravy would flow from one side of his plate to the other.

"William," Mom said. "Food is to eat, not to play with."

I guess if you took a poll of the most used sentences around our house, that would be about No. 3, and it got the conversation back to safe ground.

I was surprised at how relieved I felt, but it was premature because Dad said, "I didn't know you were in a play, Janine." I might have known he'd pick up on that because he occasionally acted in community theater productions.

I worked up a fake casual voice. "I'm not sure I *will* be. I couldn't sleep yesterday when I went up to take a nap, so I was saying lines in case I try out for a part. William and Anna Mae heard me."

"Funny time to start on a play," Dad said. "A couple of weeks before school lets out."

"Oh, did I say *school* play?" I said hastily. "It's the Summer Playhouse that's doing it. Or thinking of doing it."

William looked up from his canal building. "You said *school* when you told me and Anna Mae about it."

"Oh well," I said. "You know how confused I am these days." I touched my head to indicate that things weren't back in good working order yet. "William, let's . . ."

"Are you going to be Romeo or Juliet?" William interrupted.

Dad looked puzzled. "The Summer Playhouse is doing a *Shakespeare* play? Maybe I'll try out, too."

Could the murder of a little brother be considered justifiable homicide? I wished I could at least tape William's mouth shut.

He hadn't finished. Leaning toward me he said softly, "Anna Mae says you're not so good when you're playing Janine, but that you're super when you're Lenore."

The phone rang.

"I'll get it," I yelled, stumbling over the leg of my chair in my haste. It wasn't until I was lifting the receiver of the phone that I replayed William's last remark and realized just what he'd said.

I could barely speak through a suddenly dry throat. "Hello?"

"Hello?" It was Scott's mother. "Janine, Scott's worse."

My throat went even drier. "Worse?"

"His temperature is very high. Some kind of infection."

"Is there anything I can do?"

"No," Mrs. Nelson said. "They're letting only close relatives in to see him."

I gripped the receiver. "I know. I went to the hospital yesterday. They told me I couldn't see him." Suddenly I felt guilty about not having called to find out how he was. I'd been so snarled up in my problems with Lenore and the bracelet and Rafe that I'd forgotten.

How could I possibly forget Scott?

"I'll tell him you were there." Mrs. Nelson's voice was ragged with worry. "And I'll let you know when you can see him." She sighed. "He worries a lot about you. He says it's all his fault that you got hurt."

I'd planted that thought, or at least nourished it, with the slips of my tongue. "Tell him I'm fine, Mrs. Nelson. Tell him I'll be in to see him as soon as he's able to have visitors."

"Thanks, Janine. He'll be glad to hear from you."

She hung up.

Lenore spoke as I replaced the receiver. *"Don't tell Mom and Dad about Scott. They'll wonder why you're still going out if you aren't stopping by the hospital."*

"I'm not going out." This time I was careful to speak to Lenore inside my head. *"I can't, not with Scott so sick."*

"If you cancel the date, you'll have to sit around here and explain how come you're trying out for a play that isn't going to happen," Lenore said. *"And you'll have to figure out how to explain William's remark about Janine and Lenore."*

I thought about it.

Lenore had won again.

"That was Rafe," I told my family back in the dining room. "He's going to be a few minutes early so I'd better scoot upstairs and get ready."

Without finishing my dinner, I went upstairs to my room where the first thing I saw was the blue bracelet, lying on my dresser where I'd left it.

If Scott could have no visitors, there was no way I could explain to Rafe why we had to stop by the hospital.

The bracelet was not going to get back to its tray in the gift shop that night.

What was happening to me? Was I a criminal now?

TEN

Standing in front of my mirror again, I looked closely at my reflection. Perhaps gazing at myself would give me some indication of what was happening. The Janine I used to know wouldn't be tangled in this snarl of lies.

It was Lenore's fault.

Lowering my eyes to Mom's painting of Lenore and me that I'd propped against my mirror, I tried to see some difference in the two little girls' faces. Wasn't there something sinister there in Lenore's eyes even then, when we were babies? If she had grown up, wouldn't she have been the evil twin while I was the good one?

But the two little faces were identical. Sweet. Innocent.

Lifting the painting, I held it up to the mirror with the painted image of Janine just below my face. I raised my chin just a little, then turned my head slightly toward the empty space where Lenore might have stood if she'd been there in body. It was the same pose as in the painting.

"Mom forgot something," Lenore said.

I looked closely at the painting, then at my face. There was nothing missing. "What do you mean?"

"The mole," Lenore said. *"Look under your chin, Janine."*

I did. I looked at the familiar mole under the right side of my chin.

There was no mole in the painting.

"Maybe Mom didn't want to show a blemish on her baby." Even as I spoke, I had another of those flashes that illuminated something buried deep in my mind. But it was gone before I could realize what it was.

Or was it that I didn't want to realize?

"I had a mole, too," Lenore said. *"Don't you remember?"*

"No," I said shortly. "I don't."

"You will," Lenore said.

I put the painting down as if it were hot. As I did so, my fingers briefly touched the smoothness of the blue bracelet there on my dresser. Reminder of my guilt. Symbol of what I had become.

No! Reminder of Lenore!

"Let's get ready," Lenore urged. *"Rafe will be here soon."*

"I'll get ready when I feel like it," I said in sudden fury. "You're not calling the shots, Lenore."

"Janine?" There was a tap at my door and I looked up to see Mom standing there. "Were you talking to yourself?"

"Sort of." I tried a sheepish grin, vowing for the umpteenth time to speak to Lenore only in my head.

Mom didn't question me. "I just came up to see if you need help getting dressed. Or were you planning to wear what you have on?"

The faded jeans and oversize T-shirt I wore had been all right for my visit to the hospital, but not for a date with Rafe. "No, I thought I'd wear my blue Cherokees and my blue-and-white shirt. I'd be happy for your help, Mom."

That wasn't quite the truth. I hated having to accept help with simple things like getting dressed. Still, I was grateful to Mom for wanting to help. I hurried to get the clothes from my closet.

"Oh no," I groaned, looking at the blue-and-white shirt I'd planned to wear. The sleeves were elbow length and tight. "The sleeve will never go over my cast."

"What a shame. You look so nice in blue." Mom walked across the room toward me. Passing my dresser, she spotted the blue bracelet lying there on top. "How pretty! You probably planned on wearing this with the blouse." She picked up the bracelet. "I've never seen this before. Where did you get it?"

"It belongs to Catherine," I said quickly. "She loaned it to me for a while to cheer me up."

This new lie rolled off my tongue as smoothly as syrup over a pancake.

To get Mom's mind off the bracelet, I walked over beside her. "While you're here, Mom, look at the painting." I took the bracelet from her fingers and shoved it into my jeans pocket. "Did you know you left off my mole?" I touched the mark under the right side of my chin.

126   Mom peered at the painting. "Well, I surely did. I guess it didn't show up all that well in the photograph."

"Yes, it did," I said, then wondered why I said it. Did I remember? Or had Lenore said it? No, it was there in my mind, the image of that photograph, the two little faces, chins slightly uplifted. The mole was clearly visible. Under each chin.

"Easily remedied." Mom picked up one of my eyeliner pencils, squinted at me, then touched the pencil to the painting. "Voilà, a mole!"

She held the painting up so I could see.

I reached up a hand to finger the mole under the right side of my chin. Mom had put the mole on the right side of the chin of the little girl on the left. "You put the mole on Lenore," I said, pointing at the name embroidered on the shirt of that twin.

Mom turned the canvas so she could see it. "Well, you both had moles, you know. Mirror image moles. One of you had the mole on the right side of your chin and the other had it on the left." She picked up the eyeliner pencil again and touched it to the left side of the other twin's chin. "There," she said. "It's fixed."

But it wasn't. The twin with "Janine" embroidered on her dress now had a mole under the left side of her chin.

But my mole was under the right side of my chin. It was all wrong.

Or was it?

I was suddenly choked with panic. What was it

I didn't want to remember? What hideous thing was it that skulked in my subconscious, waiting to pounce when I got close enough?

"I've got to get dressed," I said, turning to stir frantically through my closet. I yanked out a sleeveless white blouse.

"If you really want to wear the blue-and-white shirt," Mom said, "we could open up the sleeve and I could sew it shut after you have it on. That would make Scott wonder how you achieved the marvel of getting into it."

For a second I couldn't figure out why she was talking about Scott. But then I remembered that she still thought that's where Rafe and I were going tonight, to the hospital to see Scott.

"Or," Mom suggested, "you could just wear the sleeveless blouse with your blue sweater over your shoulders and highlight the whole thing with Catherine's beautiful bracelet. She won't mind if you wear it, will she?"

128

"Catherine won't mind at all if I wear it," I said, continuing the lie.

I'd planned to stay upstairs until Rafe came, just to avoid any further conversation. But then I thought of Rafe arriving, and Mom answering the door and saying something about visiting Scott in the hospital. Rafe wouldn't have a clue as to what she was talking about, and a whole new can of worms would be opened.

So I tagged along behind when Mom went downstairs.

"Rafe and I might stop somewhere for a burger or something after we visit Scott," I said, keeping up the pretense of the hospital visit. "So don't expect us home right away."

Mom groaned. "I wish I still had the stomach to take greasy fast food late at night."

She trusted me so completely that I writhed with shame.

Rafe came right on time, before William had a chance to say anything more about Lenore, before Dad discussed the fictitious play any further, before Mom questioned me any more about visiting Scott.

"I'll just run out to meet him," I said as Rafe's car stopped in front of our house. "To save time. Visiting hours and all, you know."

"I wish you'd bring him in so we could meet him," Mom said.

But I was already out the door.

Rafe was heading up the walk to meet me. "I would have come in to get you, Janine. I'm not one of those guys who sits out in the car and honks." He stepped back to gaze at me. "Wow, you look terrific."

Talk about terrific! Rafe was the one who looked terrific. He wore beige pants and a burnt orange shirt that was just right with his dark auburn hair. He'd left his crutches home.

It was as if he'd dressed for a special occasion.

A special occasion, going out with me? Not movie-star-handsome Rafe Belmont, with his reputation for being a stud.

But of course it was Lenore he'd wanted to be with.

Lenore must have been thinking the same thing. "*Okay,*" she said. "*You can check out now.*"

"*What do you mean, check out?*" I was very careful to speak inside my head.

"*Just what I said. This is my date. You're just along to provide the vehicle.*"

She made it sound as if my body were a car and I was driving her somewhere in it.

"*Now wait a minute, Lenore. I've been really nice to you the last couple of days, but if you think I'm just going to fade away and let you take over completely, you're crazy.*"

Lenore chuckled. "*I can do it, you know, whether you want me to or not.*"

I felt the panic that was becoming familiar to me these days. *"No, you can't. I'm still in control."*

"Want me to show you?" she asked. *"Want me to pick your nose or scratch your armpit or something really gross right here in front of Rafe?"*

"Lenore," I cried. *"I wouldn't have come on this date at all if I'd known you were going to pull something like this."*

She chuckled again. *"Yes, you would have. You wanted this date as much as I did. Now just relax and enjoy it."*

What could I do? Lenore might very well be strong enough now to take over.

"Okay, Lenore," I said. *"It's your date. But we're going to talk about this later."*

Rafe was offering a hand to help me into his low-slung little sports car. Red, which seemed right for him.

After I was settled, he ran around to the other side and slid in under the wheel. He'd no sooner started the engine than Lenore leaned across the small space between the bucket seats and put my left arm, the unbroken one, through his.

"How fast can this little car go?" she asked, smiling up into his face.

Rafe looked surprised. "As fast as you want it to go."

"Show me," Lenore said.

The puzzlement remained on Rafe's face for a couple of seconds, then he grinned. "All RIGHT."

He stomped on the gas pedal, and we peeled out of there going really fast. I hoped Mom and Dad weren't watching.

"Let me know if you see any cop cars," Rafe said.

We rolled through a stop sign and hurtled along toward a changing light in the next block. Memories of another intersection roared into my mind and I would have screamed except that Lenore was using my machinery to yell, "Go for it! It's barely pink."

Rafe gunned the car through the red light. "You amaze me, Janine," he said. "You're like two girls in one." We shot onto the freeway like a guided missile. "Where are we headed?"

"What are the choices?"

"Anywhere you want to go, babe. Make a wish and I'll grant it."

"*What should I say?*" Lenore asked urgently inside my head. "*I don't know what's available.*"

She had weakened momentarily, so I took over. "Magic Mountain," I said firmly. "I like the rides." I also liked the safety of crowds.

Rafe grinned. "I could take you to our own

Magic Mountain. We can go up Angeles Crest Highway to my favorite spot where you can see the whole world. Just you and me, alone, with the big, big sky above us." He looked into my eyes. "How about it?"

Lenore had gathered enough strength to take over again. "Maybe," she said with a sideways smile at Rafe.

"*Lenore!*" I yelled. "*We're not going up on Angeles Crest. You have no idea what you'd be getting into.*"

"*I'm willing to find out,*" she said.

"*Well, I'm not.*" I was getting agitated and I had to keep reminding myself to speak inside my head. "*Look, you can pick or scratch or whatever gross things you want to do, but I'm not going up on Angeles Crest with Rafe Belmont. I'll fight you if you tell him you'll do that.*"

"Well, what's it to be?" Rafe was getting impatient. "I have to know where to guide this bomb."

"Magic Mountain it is," Lenore said. She held up my right arm in its cast. "I have to be a little careful with this."

For just a breath Rafe looked puzzled, but then he grinned. "Okay, Janine," he said softly. "We'll leave Angeles Crest for another time. How's that?"

"Way to go," Lenore said.

"Lenore, you don't even know what you're promising. There's no way I'd keep that kind of date." I tried to keep my voice stern, but as Rafe whipped the little car off the freeway to turn in the other direction, I could hardly suppress a shiver of excitement.

ELEVEN

Lenore was dazzled by Magic Mountain, like a little kid.

"I want to try everything!" she cried with my voice, controlling my body. Controlling *me*.

"Well, we'd better get going then," Rafe said. "The park closes in a few hours." He took my arm and steered me in the direction of a ride that did a complete loop-the-loop. "We'll start with this and work up to the roller coaster over there. It's a killer."

"Great," Lenore said. "I'm ready for anything."

Rafe grinned down at me—or at her—and his snapping eyes said things I didn't care to read.

But Lenore had promised to behave, so I let her take control, not so much to please her as to ease my conscience. It wasn't I who was there with Rafe. It was Lenore.

I knew what Dr. Zeigler would say. She'd tell me I was just showing another aspect of my own personality. She'd say I *wanted* to be there with Rafe but didn't want to admit it.

"You're wrong," I'd say back to her, even though I knew she could be right.

I still had to do the walking since Lenore couldn't seem to coordinate everything at once. I was happy enough to do that because that way she couldn't take me anywhere I wasn't willing to go.

The waiting line at the first ride was long. We tacked ourselves on to the end of it, standing there face-to-face with Rafe's arms slung low around my waist the way a dozen other young couples stood. My cast was there between us, though, keeping me from being pressed too closely against his chest.

But was that good news or bad?

Rafe spoke in a soft, smooth voice and Lenore answered, saying frivolous little things that made him laugh, the sound resonating deep in his chest. I hardly heard what they said. I was concentrating on Scott, telling myself that as long as I kept my thoughts on him I need not feel guilty about being there or about liking the way Rafe's body felt against mine or about watching the way Rafe's lips moved to form the words he was saying to Lenore.

I had been to Magic Mountain many times before, but never with anybody like Rafe. When we finally got on the little car, he eased me close against his side as we swooped around the curves and hung upside down for a fraction of a second.

"Go for it!" he yelled, and Lenore echoed, "Go for it!"

I was scared, not because the ride was dangerous but because Rafe was. Dangerous and wild and totally exhilarating.

I think I was more scared of the drive home than of any of the rides at Magic Mountain.

"I'm really tired," I said, grabbing control from Lenore who had weakened from fatigue.

Rafe nosed the little car into the traffic leaving the parking lot. "What gives? There's a lot of the night left."

I felt Lenore struggle to take over, but I was stronger.

I shook my head. "Not for me. You know how it is when excitement keeps you going until you relax for a minute, then you're totally thrashed."

"We could bring the excitement back," Rafe suggested.

I held up my plaster-encased arm. "I think you'd better take me home."

Lenore had been sputtering all during the conversation and now she said inside my head, *"What's the big idea? You told me this was my night, and I don't want to go home. I've been behaving."*

"Do you call it behaving when you lead Rafe on all night? With a guy like him, that's just asking for trouble."

"I can handle him," Lenore sulked.

"You don't have the faintest idea how to handle him. And neither do I," I admitted.

Lenore snorted. *"You're chicken."*

"Yes, I am." To Rafe I said, "I'm sorry."

"So am I." He glanced at me quizzically as he stopped for a red light just before the freeway. "You know what's funny, Janine? All night it's been like I've been out with two different girls."

He'd said practically the same thing earlier.

Gunning the little car, he shot it onto the freeway heading for home while Lenore wailed her displeasure inside my head.

Rafe walked me to the door when we got to my house, then stood there looking down at me. Was he deciding whether to kiss me or not? He had a reputation for taking what he wanted.

Did I hope he would or hope he wouldn't?

There was no question about Lenore.

"Let him kiss me." It was almost a plea.

I looked at his full lips with the strong, even teeth behind them and thought about the way they would feel against mine. I thought about him pulling me close to him the way we'd stood in the line and wondered if I could put my arm with the cast behind him some way so that the whole length of him would be pressed against me.

It was the cast that decided me. Maybe it reminded me of the accident. And of Scott. Or maybe it was just because I was fearful of being awkward with it.

Or maybe it was because Rafe hesitated a second too long. At any rate, I turned to open the door saying, "Thanks, Rafe. I really enjoyed the evening."

I could have been a sixth-grader thanking a spindly kid for an afternoon movie.

Rafe smiled. "You're a cool one, Janine." He leaned over and his lips brushed my forehead. Then he turned to go.

"You've ruined it all with your prissy little ways," Lenore wailed.

"Ruined what, Lenore? You've had your date with him. Now it's all over."

But then Rafe stopped. He stood for a moment, then turned back to say, "Want to go out with me Sunday, Janine? It's the Memorial Day holiday Monday, so we don't have to get in early."

"I'd like that, Rafe," Lenore said quickly.

Opening the front door, I slid inside and leaned against it.

"Janine?" Mom called from the family room.

"Yes, Mom." I thought about sneaking upstairs without facing Mom and Dad. I should have called them from Magic Mountain to say I'd be later than expected. But I hadn't even given them a thought.

No, that wasn't true. I *had* thought about calling. After all, I was Janine, the good girl, the thoughtful, considerate twin.

Why then hadn't I done it?

Before I could go anywhere, Mom came running out with Dad looming right behind her.

"Janine, we were almost ready to call the police. Where have you been?" Mom came up and put her arms around me. Her face looked pale and pinched.

"Did you have car trouble or something?" Dad asked. "We called the hospital when you didn't come home and they said Scott couldn't have visitors, as I'm sure you found out when you got there. We've been worried." He, too, came over to touch me as if to reassure himself that I was there in the flesh.

A fresh lie bubbled to my lips. But when I looked into their concerned faces, I couldn't say it. I was *Janine*. The *good* twin.

"We went to Magic Mountain," I said. "We did it on impulse."

"Honey," Mom shook her head as she spoke, "we don't know this Rafe at all. We imagined all kinds of hideous things."

Dad was more stern. "I believe they have telephones at Magic Mountain."

I tried on a contrite look. "I'm sorry. I guess I was cooped up in that hospital too long. Being free is like getting out of prison. I guess I freaked out."

"That's good, Janine," Lenore praised. *"They won't ground us after that one."*

She thought I was just conning Mom and Dad. *"Oh, shut up, Lenore. I'm not doing it just to get off the hook."*

But maybe I was. How could I be sure anymore?

My trusting father accepted the explanation.

"It's all right," he said while Mom watched me with narrowed eyes. "You're home safely now. But please, Janine, don't scare us like that again."

It wasn't likely. I wasn't planning to let Lenore take such complete control again.

"I'll make you some hot cocoa," Mom said finally. "It will help you relax so you can sleep."

I let myself be escorted into the kitchen where Boomer slept under the table. He woke and flopped his tail at me, recognizing that this was Janine, good old familiar *dull* Janine.

Dutifully I drank the cocoa. I didn't feel as if I needed anything to help me sleep. All I really wanted to do was close my eyes and drift away from the thoughts of Rafe that crowded my head. Or was it *to* Rafe that I wanted them to drift?

When I finally got up to my room, Lenore wanted to talk.

"I've been wondering," she said softly. *"What does a kiss feel like?"*

I pinned my thoughts on kissing Scott, which I hadn't done yet. The longed-for kiss at the beach had been postponed because of the accident.

"It depends on who you're kissing," I said. *"My first kiss was from Homer Selkirk at a spin-the-bottle party in the sixth grade. His lips were all chapped since he'd been out in the sun a lot and it was like kissing a piece of sandpaper. Then there was Randy DeMars in the eighth grade. He kissed like a Saint Bernard."*

"What's the big deal about kissing then?" Lenore asked. "Why does everybody make such a fuss about it?"

"I haven't told you about the good ones yet." I didn't think it was necessary to mention that the only other guy I'd ever kissed was Dave Hayes. But he was good. He kissed as if he'd had experience.

I walked over to my dresser mirror and looked into my own eyes. "When it's somebody you like, Lenore, you feel all warm and cozy and it's exciting just being close to him." I thought about Rafe. "Then when he moves in and bends his head, you open your mouth just a little."

I tipped my chin up as if I were about to receive a kiss. That brought the mole under my chin into view, and again I had one of those flashes about the photo. This flash had something to do with the attic. Was it there?

But when I tried to grab the memory of just what was in the attic, it slipped away again.

How could I know where the photo was, anyway? It had been missing for years, Mom said, and even she didn't know where it was. Why would I know?

"And then what?" Lenore asked. "What comes next?"

Intruder! Suddenly I was angry at her again. I wanted to get rid of her, send her back to that place where she'd been.

She wanted to experience life. Well, I would let her do that so she'd go.

"*Okay, Lenore,*" I said. "*Maybe I'll let you kiss Rafe on Sunday night. Then you'll know what it's like.*"

Then I would know, too.

TWELVE

The next morning I decided to look for the picture of Lenore and me that kept flashing in my memory.

I didn't bother looking in any of the boxes I kept stored in my closet. I'd cleaned out my closet when I was twelve, when I'd decided it was time to put my childhood away. I'd packed together my dolls, *Highlights* magazines, and grade-school pictures and put them in the little attic room we used for storage. The photo of Lenore and me could be there.

It wasn't easy for me to get to the attic room. I had to pull down a ladder and climb up, and then there wasn't much space. But I didn't want help. I needed to conduct my search alone.

The boxes I found hadn't been opened since I'd

put them there. They were covered with dust that gave me a sneezing fit.

Lenore didn't like it.

"Do we have to stay up here?" she asked after I lifted the lid of a large box marked DOLLS and sneezed several times. *"What are you looking for, anyway?"*

"If you must know, I'm trying to find a picture of us. You and me."

"What do you want that for?" Lenore sounded faintly suspicious. *"Isn't it the same as Mom's painting?"*

I stirred around inside the box. *"Yes. But I keep having memories of the original picture, and I'd like to find it."*

As I spoke I lifted my old Barbie doll from the box. Underneath her was a stack of her tiny dresses and boots and some other things Mom had made for her.

I looked at her briefly and was putting her back into the box when Lenore objected. *"Don't put her back yet. I want to see her. Let's play with her for a while."*

Lenore was such a child.

But to be truthful, I was tempted, too. I'd missed Barbie over the years since I'd last seen her.

But I said, *"I'm too old to be playing with dolls, Lenore."*

"Oh, please," she said. *"Look at those darling clothes. Just let me dress her up in some of those cute things."*

So what could it hurt? She'd missed those years. Maybe she needed to catch up, like a makeup exam at school. Maybe she needed a quick run-through of that period of my life.

I let Lenore dress and undress the doll several times by holding her with the stiff fingers of my broken arm while she maneuvered the tiny garments on and off with the other hand.

While she played, I tried to remember what was in the other boxes. Now that I was up in the attic, I had the feeling that it wasn't the right place to look after all. I'd gone through all that stuff before storing it. I would have remembered the picture if I'd seen it at the time, wouldn't I?

On the other hand, it could possibly be in one of my grade-school scrapbooks, couldn't it?

147

Lenore wasn't ready to give up the Barbie doll yet, so I had to wait until she'd tried on every single article of clothing in the box. Then she discovered a Ken doll underneath the Barbie clothes and she had to have a fashion show for him as well.

I can't say I didn't enjoy reliving my childhood.

But finally I took control again. *"I came up here to look for the picture,"* I said when Lenore objected. Shoving the dolls back in the box and closing it, I shifted over to another box marked SCRAPBOOKS.

"Poop," grumbled Lenore. *"Why can't we ever do anything I want to do?"*

"We just did," I snapped. *"Besides, whose body is this, anyway? And don't say* poop." I sounded just like Mom.

"William says it."

"William is eight years old. It's the kind of thing an eight-year-old says." I yanked open the scrapbook box and let go another volley of sneezes.

"Poop." Lenore sighed. *"You're sure hard to live with."*

I didn't even bother to answer that one. Picking up a scrapbook, I flipped through it, somehow knowing the photo wasn't there.

"Wait," Lenore cried. *"Let me see some of that stuff."*

"Not now, Lenore." I put the scrapbook back in the box. *"It's just full of old school pictures and stuff like that."*

"That's why I want to see it," she said. *"I want*

to see what you were like. What I might have been like."

"Forget it. You wouldn't have been anything like me." I felt around in the bottom of the box to see if there might be any loose pictures there. The only thing I found was a pair of old scissors, the blunt kind that little kids use. That's what I'd used to cut pictures out of the Sears catalog when I was little.

As I picked up the scissors and fitted my fingers into the proper places, I was zapped by another of those weird flashes, but this one was almost like an electric shock. I remembered cutting something with those scissors. Something about which I'd been very upset.

I was still staring at the scissors when I heard William coming up the ladder. He came up nimbly because he was a tree climber and a fence scaler, agile as a monkey.

"Hi." His head appeared through the opening in the floor. "Whatcha doing here?"

"Hi," Lenore said aloud before I could change my focus away from the scissors. "We're just looking through some old stuff."

William looked at me curiously. "What do you mean 'we'? Is somebody up here with you?"

I think he would have accepted it without question if I'd said yes, there is. But Lenore decided to be playful. Dropping my voice to a mysterious whisper, she said, "Would you believe there are two little people in that box over there?" She twitched my head toward the Barbie and Ken box.

It was time for me to take over again. It wasn't nice to tease William that way. I struggled, but Lenore was becoming too strong.

William's eyes shifted to the box, then back to me. "How little?"

"About this high." Lenore held my left hand about a foot from the floor.

"You're kidding." William watched me, and I wasn't sure all of his interest had to do with the foot-high people.

Exerting all my will, I pushed past Lenore. "Yes, I *am* kidding," I said. "You know we don't keep little people in boxes in the attic."

It was Lenore's turn to exert will. "Yes, we do, William." Snaking out my good arm, she pulled the doll box over close to me. "Wouldn't you like to see them?"

His eyes fixed on me, William took a step backward down the ladder. "I don't think so." Backing down a couple more steps, he jumped to the floor and ran for the stairs. "Ma-a-a-a-a-a!" he bellowed.

"Now you've done it," I accused Lenore. *"He's going to go blabbing to Mom that there's something weird going on here. He knows you're here, you know."*

"Yes," Lenore said. *"I was just teasing. I thought he might like to play with the Barbie and Ken dolls."*

"Well, you didn't have to tell him there were little people in that box. He's always been scared of the attic."

"Well, how was I to know that?"

I was furious with Lenore. I wished I could cut her out of me with those blunt scissors just the way I had cut her out of the picture of her and me.

Cut her out of the picture! There it was, the knowledge I'd had lurking somewhere in the dark places of my brain. Now I knew why the scissors had made me flash on it. I had cut the picture. I had tried to destroy it.

Why would I cut the photograph of Lenore and me?

"Janine," Mom called. She was at the foot of the ladder. I hadn't heard her come up the carpeted stairs. "Janine, William said there's somebody up there with you."

I stood up. I couldn't tell Mom about the picture yet. Not until I remembered why I'd cut it.

I managed a squeaky little fake laugh. "There's nobody here with me, Mom. I was just talking to myself."

"But William said . . ."

I interrupted her. "Remember that play I wanted to try out for? I was just going over lines."

Now Mom laughed, too. "You know what William said? He said there were two of you up there and that both of you had talked to him."

"Two parts, Mom. I thought I might as well try out for two different parts."

"That William!" Mom said affectionately. "Janine, I was wondering if you'd like to check with the hospital and see if Scott can have visitors today. I'm going to the hospital to see Mrs. Kimberly. She had an emergency gallbladder operation last night."

"Sorry to hear that. I'll go with you to the hospital, Mom. If Scott can't have visitors, I'll visit Hallie."

This was my chance to take the blue bracelet back to the gift shop.

We left William and Dad doing Saturday chores. They were watering Dad's summer vegetable garden, already green and flourishing in the late May heat.

"It must have been a disappointment when you couldn't see Scott last night," Mom said as we drove toward the hospital. "Are he and Rafe good friends?"

"They got to be good friends while they were roommates at the hospital," I said.

I wished she hadn't mentioned Rafe. It made me recall my promise to Lenore—that I would let him kiss me Sunday night.

Kiss *Lenore,* that is. Scott was the only guy I wanted to kiss *me.*

Then why did the thought of Rafe make me shiver?

Nervously, I twisted the blue bracelet that I'd slipped onto my arm under a blouse with long, full sleeves. I'd rolled the right sleeve up above my cast, but I needed that long sleeve on the other arm to cover up the bracelet.

"Are you cold?" Mom asked, reaching out to turn off the car's air-conditioning.

"No. I guess I was just thinking of the hospital. I don't like that place."

"We won't stay long," Mom assured me. "I'll meet you at the gift shop after we've both made our visits."

When we got to the hospital, Mom went off toward the surgical floor and I headed once more for orthopedics. I worried as I rode the elevator to the fifth floor. What if Scott had heard I'd been out with Rafe the night before?

But that was silly. Nobody had seen us.

I was hoping the same warm, friendly nurse I'd spoken with before would be at the desk, but there was a different one. This one looked coldly at me when I asked if Scott was in his room.

"Are you a relative?"

I shook my head.

"Family visits only," she stated.

"Can you just tell me if he's back in his room? He wasn't there on Thursday."

"He's back. No visitors. Except family."

I looked toward the closed door of Scott's room. "I'm not family, but I was in the same accident as he was." I held up my plastered arm.

She squinted at it, then sighed as if I were making her life very difficult. "Well, just five minutes. He needs his rest."

"Thank you," I mumbled, heading for Room 502.

"*A real dragon,*" Lenore commented. "*I thought all nurses smiled and called people 'dear.'*"

"*You've just been lucky, Lenore. There are all kinds of people in the world.*"

"I thought being nice went with the job."

Who was she to criticize? *"Maybe she has problems. Maybe her husband left her with five kids to support. Maybe she has bunions. Not everybody gets a free ride like you do, Lenore."*

"Hey, do you think it's all fun and games traveling with you?"

I wished again that I could cut her out of the picture, neatly separating her from me so that I once more stood alone. Alone, like the half of that photograph.

When had I cut that picture? Had it been *before* the accident that killed Lenore? Could I actually have been somehow responsible for her death? No, no, not at four years of age. That was too ludicrous even to consider.

"Be quiet now, Lenore," I instructed. Taking a deep breath, I walked to Scott's door and pushed it open.

He was lying flat in bed. The TV was on, but he wasn't watching it. He smiled when he saw me, but mostly he just looked sick.

155

"Hi, Scott." I didn't know what else to say.

"Hi." He reached a hand toward me and I took hold of it. "There must be a fairy godmother fluttering around here somewhere. I was wishing you'd come, and here you are."

"I was here on Thursday, too. You weren't here."

"Thursday?" He frowned, trying to recall Thursday. "I guess I'm still foggy about that day."

"I'm sorry you've had such a hard time, Scott."

"I'm going to be okay." He smiled. "You look great. I guess you're feeling better."

I smiled back at him. "Just waiting for you to get out of here so we can finish that trip to the beach."

His eyes brightened. "Can we really do that, Janine? That was going to be such a good day." He tugged gently at my hand, pulling me toward him.

"He's going to kiss you," Lenore said.

I drew back. Lenore's kiss was coming on Sunday night. I didn't want her sharing mine.

I hesitated a fraction of a second too long. A pained look crossed Scott's face and he dropped his hand to the bed.

"Scott," I began.

156   "It's okay, Janine. I understand. It's going to take you a while to forgive me for that trip."

"No, no," I protested. "That's not it at all."

The icy nurse opened the door.

"Time's up," she said. "You'll have to leave."

She stood there holding the door open.

"That seemed like a short five minutes," I said. "Well . . . good-bye, Scott."

Scott waved to me, but he didn't ask me to come back.

I didn't see Mom anywhere when I got to the gift shop. That was fine. The blue bracelet had been burning a groove in my arm all during my visit with Scott. I wanted to get rid of it.

I circulated around the gift shop for a few minutes, picking up things and looking as if I might be considering buying them. There was no one except for the clerk in the shop, and she was watching me too closely for me to put the bracelet back on the tray. I don't think she suspected me of anything. She just wanted to be helpful, telling me she had different varieties of stationery under the counter and some books she hadn't yet put out.

Another customer came in, and I had my chance. I headed for the tray from which Lenore had taken the bracelet. I slid it off my arm and was just replacing it on the tray when I looked up, straight into Mom's startled eyes.

THIRTEEN

"Janine," Mom said, "what are you doing?"

Now was the time to tell the truth.

Forget Dr. Zeigler's multiple personality theory. Mom would know that I would never steal a bracelet, then try to sneak it back. It was time to name Lenore as the thief, to tell Mom again that Lenore was here, that she was messing up my life.

But before I could say a thing, Lenore swung into action.

"Isn't this a coincidence?" she said smoothly with my voice. "This bracelet is just like the one Catherine loaned me."

More proof of Lenore's presence. I had never been glib like that.

Mom's eyes locked onto mine. "Is it? It looks like the same bracelet to me."

"No, look." Lenore picked up the blue bracelet. "See? These little flowers have yellow petals, and on Catherine's the petals are white."

Mom looked at the bracelet. She was quiet for several seconds. Then she said, "I don't remember it that well, I guess."

The habit of trusting me was too strong. I knew she believed what Lenore was saying.

The saleswoman came over and smiled questioningly at me.

Lenore slipped the bracelet back onto my arm. "I just love this," Lenore said. "My best friend has one just like it."

The saleswoman looked puzzled. "I didn't know we had any blue bracelets left. They were very popular. Where did you find that one?"

"It was under the edge of the tray," Lenore lied. "I guess somebody knocked it off."

"It's the last one, then," the saleswoman said. "May I wrap it for you?"

"Oh, I'd really love it," Lenore said. "But I'm afraid it's too expensive."

"Go ahead if you like it, Janine," Mom said. "We'll call it a get-well gift." Opening her purse, she took out her wallet.

"Oh, Mom, thanks." Lenore was ecstatic. "I love it. I've never had a bracelet before."

Mom handed the saleswoman some bills. "What do you mean you've never had a bracelet before? What about the gold one your grandmother gave you? And that nice one Dad and I gave you for your eleventh birthday?"

Lenore realized her mistake and started stammering. It was my turn to take over. Now I could tell Mom the truth.

But all I said was, "You know what I mean. It's the first one I've ever picked out for myself."

"That's true." Mom collected her change and we left the shop with the blue bracelet, now cool and smooth on my arm.

When we got home, I headed upstairs to my room. I was going to confront Lenore. But confront her with what? I'd had my chance to end the whole bracelet thing, and I'd failed.

In the upstairs hallway I found that the ladder to the attic was down, and William was standing
halfway up on it.

"Hey, kiddo, what're you doing?" I asked.

William looked around guiltily. "Anna Mae's up there." He pointed to the attic.

Anna Mae poked her head through the attic hole. "Hi. William told me that Lenore told him there were little people up here. I can't find them nowhere."

"I was just kidding when I told him that, Anna Mae." I motioned for her to come down.

Anna Mae looked at me owlishly through the thick lenses of her glasses. "Not you. Lenore. William said she was the one who told him."

William hid his face against the ladder.

"William, I was the only person up there in the attic." I put my hand on his back and rubbed it a little.

He squirmed under my hand, but he didn't say anything.

"It's okay to tell me. Did you think there was somebody up there with me?"

He darted a quick little glance at me, then ducked his head again. "Yes. The one named Lenore."

William didn't know what to do with his knowledge. I didn't want to deny what he knew because I might need him to back me up when I decided to tell Mom and Dad about Lenore. But I also didn't want him and Anna Mae telling other people that Lenore and I spoke together. It wasn't time yet.

"William, do you know who Lenore is?" I asked.

He shook his head.

The light glinted off Anna Mae's glasses as she watched with interest. "Is she somebody spooky?"

I laughed. "No, Anna Mae. Not at all. Come on down and I'll show you who she is. And by the way, the little people in the attic are just my old Barbie and Ken dolls. They're in a box up there marked DOLLS. Can you see it?"

Anna Mae's head disappeared from the attic hole.

"*You can't tell those kids about me,*" Lenore said.

"*Why not?*" I asked. "*They're kids. They still believe in Santa Claus and the Tooth Fairy. Why wouldn't they believe in Lenore, the girl who talks with my voice?*"

Lenore subsided for a moment, then said, "*How much are you going to tell them?*"

I was angry. "*Does it worry you, Lenore? Does it bother you that they know you're here?*"

"*Just be careful what you say,*" Lenore grumbled. "*You can't trust kids.*"

There were scuffling noises coming from the attic. Apparently Anna Mae was searching through my boxes.

"These are really neat," she called. "Can me

and William play with Barbie and Ken sometime, Janine?"

"I don't play with dolls," William protested.

Anna Mae's jean-clad legs appeared on the ladder as she started down. "Yes you do. You play with dolls all the time when we pretend we're married and they're our babies."

"I'd rather play Monopoly," William muttered, obviously embarrassed that now I knew he had secrets, too.

Poor henpecked William.

"I put Barbie and Ken back in the box," Anna Mae said as we hoisted the ladder back into place.

"That's fine, Anna Mae," I told her. "And yes, I'll let you play with them sometime." I led the two of them into my room where I pointed at Mom's painting of Lenore and me.

"That's Lenore, William," I said. "The little girl on the left. She was our sister. My twin. Mom has told you about her."

"Yeah," William said. "She's dead."

I nodded. "You know how when you and Anna Mae play with dolls you pretend they're talking but it's really you?"

"Yes."

"Sometimes I pretend Lenore is still with me and that we talk to each other."

Anna Mae narrowed her eyes. "You told us you were practicing for a play."

Sometimes I wished Anna Mae weren't so smart.

"I know. I didn't want anybody to know I still pretend." I lowered my voice, leaning closer to William and Anna Mae. "I'd feel dumb if Mom and Dad or anybody else knew that I pretend. So this will be our secret. Just the three of us. Okay?"

Anna Mae's eyes were huge behind the thick glasses. I couldn't tell what she was thinking. "Can we cut our fingers and make a blood pact?" she said.

"Let's just raise our right hands and swear we'll never reveal the secret." I raised my cast as high as I could.

William and Anna Mae solemnly raised their right hands. I knew William wouldn't be spilling anything because he wouldn't want me to tell anybody he played with dolls.

"We swear," he and Anna Mae said together. I could tell they felt important, making a secret pact with me.

"This is fun," Anna Mae whispered. She peered intently at the painting of Lenore and me. "Were you just exactly alike?"

"My mother said we were mirror images." I explained that meant we were reflections of each other, that the left side of my face was just like the right side of Lenore's and vice versa.

Anna Mae gazed at the painting. "Then this spot under your chin is on the wrong side," she announced. She pointed to the little girl who wore the shirt embroidered with "J-a-n-i-n-e." The little girl who had a mole under the left side of her chin while my mole was under the right side.

I felt chilly. The mole on my painted image *was* on the wrong side. That's what had made me shiver that day when Mom had picked up my eyeliner pencil and put the spot on Lenore's right side.

"Mom put it on the wrong side," I said quickly.

But now several memories came together: the mole on the wrong side, the blunt little scissors cutting the photograph in two, the hiding of the two halves. Where had I hidden them?

I had to find that photograph. I had to remember why I had cut it in two.

Then perhaps I would know what I had done to my twin sister.

165

All night long I tried to sneak up on the hidden memories of the picture. But all night long they eluded me.

I woke up on Sunday feeling sluggish and out of

sorts. I hoped I wouldn't have dark circles under my eyes for Lenore's date with Rafe.

But when I got dressed in a blue-flowered blouse and my best white pants with the blue bracelet on my arm, I looked all right.

Mom and Dad had objected when I'd told them I was going out with Rafe again, and Mom had asked what about Scott. I'd said a little stiffly that it wasn't as if I was going steady with Scott or anything like that. "In fact," I'd said, "if I did that, you'd object and say I should go out with a lot of guys."

Mom had said, "You're right," and had dropped it, much to my relief.

William invited Anna Mae to come and see that the actual, real, live Rafe Belmont was truly coming to our house to pick me up. They were both there, noses pressed to the living-room window, when he arrived promptly at four o'clock.

"See?" William said. "I told you he was coming."

Anna Mae looked impressed. "Which one's he coming to see? Janine or Lenore?"

Mom and Dad were in the family room watching TV so they didn't hear her.

"Anna Mae," I said severely. "Remember what

I told you about our secret? Nobody else is supposed to know that sometimes I pretend to be Lenore."

Anna Mae turned owl eyes at me. "I think Rafe Belmont would like Lenore best."

"That's right," Lenore said. "Rafe is *my* date."

She took over my body, my voice, my eyes as easily as slipping on a dress. When had the transition become so smooth? Was it because I was tired?

For the first time I was aware that my body was different when Lenore was controlling it. She made it stand different, straighter, maybe, with the chest poked out more than I ever did. She tipped the head just a little sideways and smiled slower and moved the eyes in a way that I never had.

Anna Mae and William both stared at me. At Lenore.

"Wow," Anna Mae breathed. "You're bee-yoo-tiful when you're Lenore."

I knew that pleased Lenore, although it didn't do much for me. But why not face it? It was Lenore Rafe had been attracted to all along, not mousy me.

On the other hand, he hadn't seen much of Lenore when he first asked me out. He'd had only a glimpse of her, that day in the hospital room when she'd given him the come-on smile. That was back in the time when that's just about all she could do.

Maybe that smile was enough to attract Rafe.

On the other hand, I was the one in control when he'd asked for the second date.

So which one of us was it that he liked?

I shooed William and Anna Mae away from the window so Rafe wouldn't see he had an audience. I was letting him come into the house this time so Mom and Dad could meet him. It might ease their minds.

But as I peeked through the curtains watching Rafe climb the steps to the porch, I didn't think anybody's mind was going to be at ease. Rafe was the best-looking guy in town. Mom had been a young girl once. She knew how it was when the "most wanted" guy went out with a girl who never would have believed she could attract that kind of guy.

I *had* to be in control that night. Suddenly it seemed to me that the blue bracelet on my arm, Lenore's bracelet, had become the symbol of her strength and my weakness, the tangible evidence of her power over me.

Before she could object, I yanked the bracelet off and dropped it into a potted plant that stood by the front door.

"Hey," Lenore said, *"I want to wear that."*

With all the energy I could pull together, I pushed Lenore aside and flung open the door. It was Janine who was going to greet Rafe. It was Janine he was going to take out tonight.

"Hi," he said, standing there on the porch like a kid calling for his first date. He looked so nice. His hair was neatly combed and his jeans were on the right side of reputable.

"Come in," I said. "Meet some admirers."

I introduced him to William and Anna Mae. William watched Rafe, but Anna Mae watched me.

"Are you up to meeting my parents?" I asked Rafe after he'd teased the two kids a little.

"I was hoping you'd introduce me," Rafe said.

He was totally polite as he met my folks. Dad stood up to shake hands and make some corny remark about how he should be careful with such precious cargo, and Mom relaxed so much that she didn't even tell us when we had to be home.

Rafe was so nice, so ordinary, that this date didn't seem any different from going out with Scott. I could be myself with him.

So why, then, did I reach down and grab the blue bracelet as we passed the potted plant on our way out? Why did I slide it back on my arm?

Anna Mae grinned at me as I went out the door. "Have a good time, Lenore," she whispered.

FOURTEEN

No, not Lenore. This time Janine was in charge.

To prove it, I suggested to Rafe that we go to the Los Angeles County Arboretum that afternoon. We would walk around, feed the ducks that swam in the lagoon, talk.

"I'd like that," Rafe said.

When we got there, he held my hand gently as we walked.

But Lenore was bored. When my arm was free, she twisted the blue bracelet. To stop her, I dropped my left arm to my side. But soon it was back up near my injured arm again, and she was twisting the bracelet around and around and around.

As we walked through the jungle surrounding

the lagoon, Rafe said, "They shoot a lot of movies and TV shows here, you know. Almost anytime you see a jungle scene, it's been done here."

I nodded. "Mom brought me here once to watch a shoot. It was fun seeing the actors."

"You know what, Janine? Sometimes I think I'd like to be an actor." Rafe leaped up onto the porch of the pretty Queen Anne house by the lagoon. "I mean, don't you think this profile would drive women crazy?" He posed, shoulders thrown back, head turned slightly so I could see the line of his nose and chin.

It drove *me* crazy, all right. But all I said was, "You stay here while I gather an audience. You shouldn't be wasting all this on just little old me."

He laughed and came down one step, making slashing motions in the air as if he carried a sword. "Maybe I could be the next Indiana Jones. Or maybe they'll make another Tarzan movie by the time I get to be a star."

"How good are you at swinging on vines?" I pointed at the jungle.

"Let's find out."

Rafe grabbed my hand and we ran like a couple of kids toward the tall trees.

"This is Dullsville," Lenore complained. *"We might as well be with Scott."*

I felt her energy surge through me, and she took over, snuggling up against Rafe as we walked into the cool dimness of the jungle. "This is more like it," she said.

Rafe seemed surprised. "I thought you were enjoying just walking around."

"I am—now." With my good arm Lenore reached back and took his hand, bringing his arm around my waist.

"Okay." Rafe tightened his arm. "Maybe it's time we split. Let's go to my favorite place."

"Just what I was thinking," Lenore murmured.

Rafe became a different person as he steered the speeding sports car around the curves of Angeles Crest Highway. He wasn't like Scott anymore, and I was afraid. Afraid of the deep canyons that chewed at the edge of the roadway. Afraid of Rafe and those bottomless dark eyes that could drown a person. Afraid of Lenore whose frustration and eagerness to live made her so strong that I was a powerless prisoner in my own body.

173

"You're going to love it up here," Rafe said.

"I know I will," Lenore drawled.

Suddenly Rafe whipped the car off the road onto a widened spot that hung over a canyon.

"Are we there already?" Lenore asked.

Rafe let the car coast to a stop but kept the motor idling. "Not yet. I thought you'd like to catch the sunset from here."

Lenore turned my head to the west where the sun was crashing in flames into the ocean. The whole western sky was ablaze with color. It was as if we had a balcony seat for a showing of the end of the world.

Lenore gasped. "I've never seen anything like that."

"I knew you'd like it, Janine." Rafe sounded pleased. "Takes your breath away, doesn't it?"

Lenore laughed deep in my throat. "I thought it was just the company that took my breath away."

Rafe gazed at me for a long moment. The fire of the sunset was reflected in those fathomless dark eyes.

Without saying anything, he twisted the steering wheel and let it inch forward a little so we were facing more south than west. From there we could see the skyscrapers of downtown Los Angeles, floating in a sea of smog. They looked like the spires of a phantom city, and from Lenore's quick inhale of breath I knew she was thinking of the same thing I was. Thinking of those pale buildings in the misty distance in that place where I had found her.

Or was it the picture on the poster in my room that it reminded me of?

For a fraction of a second Lenore weakened, but it was long enough for me to say, "Rafe, I want to go home."

He gazed at me again. "Are you sure you want to go home—Lenore?"

This time it was my turn to gasp, and Lenore snatched the chance to take over again. I knew it startled her as much as it did me to have him call her by name.

But she was smooth as butter as she said, "Why do you call me Lenore?"

Rafe laughed. "No big secret. Scott told me about your twin who died and he said you always call yourself Lenore when you're into something you don't think you ought to be doing. He said you were Lenore on the day of the accident."

"Scott likes Lenore." Lenore said it almost like a question.

"He likes Janine, too." Rafe reached over and put a hand on the side of my face. "Remember that first day when you came into our hospital room? You gave me a real come-on smile and that surprised me. After you left I told Scott I'd always thought of you as one of those sweet, shy girls, but he said sometimes you weren't all that shy. That's when he told me about how you sometimes call yourself Lenore." He gave me a slow smile. "Are you Lenore today?"

Lenore slow-smiled back. "What do you think?"

Rafe took his hand from my face and backed the car away from the edge of the cliff, then slammed it into drive. Once again we shot out onto the twisting, curving highway, heading farther back into the mountains.

"I didn't really think you wanted to go home," Rafe said.

Rafe's special place was on the edge of another canyon, near the top of Mount Wilson. From there we could see most of the Los Angeles Basin and a good part of the San Gabriel Valley. We were all alone except for a Forest Service car back by the picnic area.

Rafe rolled down the car window. "On a clear day you can see all the way to Catalina Island. It's as if the whole world is out there in front of you. Sometimes I stand here on the edge of the cliff and yell, 'Hello, everybody. Someday you're going to hear from me.'" He gave me a sheepish grin.

He was being like Scott again, boyish and nice, and I struggled to take over from Lenore. I trusted this Rafe who liked sunsets and yelled things from the edge of a cliff.

But Lenore was too strong. Turning to Rafe she said, "Did we come all the way up here to ogle the smog?"

Rafe hesitated the slightest moment, and I screamed at Lenore inside my head. *"Can't you see he's not sure about this? Can't you tell he'd rather be with me?"*

But Lenore had already moved as close to Rafe as she could in the bucket seats.

"Hel-LO, Lenore," he said in a hoarse whisper.

Lenore laughed triumphantly and settled into his arms, tipping my head to receive that first kiss.

Rafe's mouth came down on mine, hard and bruising. Lenore had had no experience but she learned fast, responding to him the way she'd seen actresses do on TV.

When Rafe came up for air he said, "This is awkward here in the car. Let's go out under the trees."

"Whatever you say," Lenore said.

Rafe opened the car door. Unfolding his legs, he got out and came around to help me.

I tried to stiffen my legs so that Lenore couldn't walk.

But she outfoxed me. "Carry me, sweets," she

said, putting up her arms. "That kiss left me too weak to walk."

Reaching into the car, Rafe picked me up as if I were a child. Effortlessly he carried me over to some tall pine trees and set me down next to a big rock on which somebody had spray-painted BIFF AND LISA WERE HERE.

"Wait a minute." Rafe sprinted back to the car.

"*Lenore,*" I said firmly. "*Let me take charge now.*"

"*No,*" she said just as firmly. "*I liked that kiss. And you did, too.*"

She was right. The kiss had been exciting in a heart-clattering way.

But it had been so demanding. So impersonal. I could have been any of the—how many?—girls Rafe had brought up here.

Rafe was coming back. He carried a blanket.

"*Lenore,*" I said. "*You don't know what you're getting into.*"

"*Oh, come on, Janine. What's the big deal?*"

Her energy kept me from fleeing back to the car.

Rafe spread the blanket out on the needle-strewn ground under the tall pines. Extending his hand, he half lifted me onto the blanket, then sat down beside me. "Are you still Lenore?"

"That's my name," Lenore whispered back.

Rafe moved in on me then, lowering me back onto the blanket. His mouth met mine again, and his hand moved against my back. Lenore put my arms around him. My right arm, in the cast, was stiff and uncomfortable, but she didn't seem to mind. She was kissing him back now, and she was doing it well.

Rafe pulled my shirt out of my jeans and I felt his warm hand against my bare skin. If he'd taken things slower, I might have responded right along with Lenore. But this was too fast. I wasn't ready for this. For any of it.

I tried to struggle, but Lenore was too strong.

I didn't hear the footsteps until they were almost by our sides.

"You kids will have to make out somewhere else," a deep voice said. It belonged to a man in a Forest Service uniform.

Rafe and I sat up abruptly. I pulled my shirt down and tried to smooth my hair. I was glad the twilight dimness hid my flaming face.

"Just watching the lights," Rafe said with a grin.

"Right." The man sounded as if he'd heard that before. "You're going to have to watch them somewhere else. This isn't the safest place in the world when night is coming on."

Lenore had been so startled by the man's arrival that she'd dropped her guard. It was easy for me to take over, and my anger made me strong enough to stay in control.

Rafe and I stood up. Rafe picked up the blanket, folding it without even shaking the pine needles from it.

"We did a drug bust here a few weeks ago," the Forest Service man said conversationally. "Stopped what could have turned out to be a murder just last month."

We were all walking toward Rafe's car. "Even people who just come up to watch the lights make problems." The ranger gestured to indicate the graffiti on the rocks and the scattered beer cans. "So we don't allow anybody to hang around this time of day. Sorry."

I wondered if Biff and Lisa had been kicked out, too.

The ride home was quiet. I tried to start a conversation, but Rafe didn't seem to want to talk.

When we got to my house he walked me to the door and stood gazing down at me for a moment with that puzzled look I'd seen before.

I gave him kind of a shaky smile as I opened the door.

"Give my regards to Janine," he said as he turned to leave.

"*You didn't even give me a chance to kiss him good-bye,*" Lenore wailed as I leaned against the closed door.

"*He didn't want to kiss you good-bye, Lenore.*"

"*How can you say that? He loves me! You were up there on the mountain, too. You know he loves me.*"

Poor Lenore. I didn't even bother to tell her that what happened up on the mountain had nothing to do with love.

FIFTEEN

Monday was the Memorial Day holiday. It was a tradition in our family to go to Rose Hills Cemetery on Memorial Day and put flowers on the graves of relatives and friends who were buried there. Mom said that's what they did in Idaho when she and Dad were growing up. She always made sure we had lots of roses and azaleas in bloom to make bouquets.

I'd never liked going to the cemetery. When I was little I'd take Catherine with me so she could decorate Lenore's grave. I never went any closer to it than I had to.

"I don't think I'll go today," I told Mom as she was getting this year's bouquets ready, wrapping newspaper cones around them to keep them nice until we got to Rose Hills.

Mom looked up from her flowers. "Janine, you have to come with us. It's not a family affair without you. Dad's going and William and even Anna Mae."

"*Let's stay home,*" Lenore said inside my head. "*Rafe might call.*"

That's what changed my mind. If Lenore wanted to stay, then I wanted to go. She had kept me awake the night before, nagging at me for not letting her give Rafe a hot kiss on the porch last night, something to bring him back panting for more. She'd railed at me for taking over so she couldn't suggest a future date herself.

If Rafe did call, which was doubtful, he'd find us not home.

Of course he could leave a message on the answering machine.

"Okay," I told Mom. "I'll go."

"Will Catherine be coming with us?" she asked.

I almost said I'd call her. But if she came, I knew Mom would make some comment about the blue bracelet that was supposed to be identical to the one I'd told her Catherine had, and poor Catherine would be mystified. Then I'd be mired in more lies.

"Not this year," I said, heading upstairs to dress.

Lenore complained when I wouldn't wear the

bracelet. There really wasn't any reason not to, except that it was a symbol of Lenore's power. Why give her an advantage?

She whined and wailed when I refused to wear it, but she couldn't take over that day. Very likely she'd spent all her energy the night before, staying in control for so long. I didn't know how those things worked with her.

I knew she was thinking about Rafe. Maybe she was depressed. Like Hallie. Like Scott.

She deserved to be depressed. She was the one who'd caused all the trouble.

As I thought about it, I knew what I was going to do when we got to the cemetery.

On the way, I sat in the backseat of our car with William and Anna Mae. Anna Mae kept watching me. As we parked at Rose Hills she leaned close to me and said, "Where's Lenore today?"

"I'll show you where she is," I whispered back. "Stay with me."

Mom was surprised when I said I wanted to take care of Lenore's flowers this year, but she handed me her prettiest bouquet of roses. Holding it in the crook of my broken arm, I hiked up the hill to the spot I'd avoided for so many years. Up the hill to Lenore's grave.

William and Anna Mae were close on my heels.

184

I found the grave without difficulty. I knew where it was. I walked up to the tiny headstone, alone among strangers, next to a tall fir tree. Mom and Dad had bought a plot when Lenore died, and nobody else in our family was there yet.

"This is where Lenore is," I said for Anna Mae's benefit. And Lenore's. "Right here."

I looked directly at the name chiseled in the stone. "Lenore Palmer," it said. Born. Died.

I felt weak.

I also felt Lenore's sudden anguish.

"No," Lenore whispered, and I knew she was taking over. Not only that, but she was speaking aloud. Then, without my realizing it, she'd reached into my jeans pocket and pulled out the blue bracelet. She put it on my arm.

When had she put it into my pocket? I tried to remember.

Maybe I was totally losing out to Lenore.

She was still speaking, and her voice sounded agitated. "No," she said again. "You shouldn't have brought me here. I'm not there in that grave. That isn't me. I'm here! I'm here! You know that!"

I felt sick and dizzy. I didn't know whether it was Lenore or I who was crying out.

But I did know suddenly what I'd done with

that photograph of Lenore and me. I didn't know yet where it was, but I knew I'd tried to hide it from myself. I'd put it away somewhere, buried it in a grave of years, just as surely as that small body was buried there in that grave before us.

I could no longer stand. I dropped limply to the ground.

Lenore went on moaning "No, no, no," and I heard startled whispers from William and Anna Mae and the sound of running feet.

Then Mom was there on her knees beside me. "Janine," she cried. "Janine, what is it?"

I heard Anna Mae's voice. Wise little owl-eyed Anna Mae. "Lenore's freaking out," she said.

Dad was there, too. "You mean Janine, Anna Mae."

"Uh-uh." I knew Anna Mae was shaking her head. "I mean Lenore."

"Anna Mae," William whispered. "Don't tell."

"Don't tell what?" Dad demanded. "What do you kids know about this?"

Neither of them said anything.

"William?" Dad's voice was firm.

I wanted to tell William to go ahead and tell everything he knew. Or suspected. It was time to tell, time to end this whole thing. If it meant being locked up in a psychiatric ward, then that was the price of it.

But Lenore was sobbing and moaning in Mom's lap. I couldn't speak or even raise my head. Lenore was keeping me from saying anything.

"Anna Mae, tell us what you know so we can help Janine," Dad said.

"Well," Anna Mae sounded reluctant, "sometimes Janine pretends to be Lenore. I think it has something to do with that play she was going to try out for in school."

I wasn't sure if Anna Mae really believed what she said or if she was just protecting Lenore. I knew she liked Lenore, ever since that day in the attic.

"Diane," Dad said to Mom, "do you know what's going on with Janine?"

There was a little lapse of time while Mom shook her head or nodded or maybe just looked blank. I couldn't see. Lenore wouldn't let me raise my head.

"She's been so focused on Lenore lately." Mom spoke as if I weren't even there. "I don't know why. I found that painting I made of the two girls, and she took it to her room. Maybe it was just too much for her to see Lenore's grave right now." She stroked my forehead with her hand, just the way she used to do when I was little. "Is that what it is, honey?"

Lenore nodded my head.

"We'd better go on home." Mom eased me from her lap. "Can you get up, Janine? Or do you want Dad to carry you?"

"I'd like Daddy to carry me," Lenore said in a high, little-girl voice.

It was all an act. I felt perfectly capable of walking, although I was still weak and shaky. But I let Dad pick me up and carry me to the car. William and Anna Mae got in the front with Dad. Mom crawled in the back with me. Lenore snuggled my body against her all the way home.

Dad carried me upstairs and put me on my unmade bed while Mom pulled down the window shades.

"My bed is so messy," Lenore said. "Why don't I just get into the guest bed."

The guest bed. The other twin bed there in my room, the one that would have been Lenore's, if she'd lived.

When I was tucked into that bed, Mom sat down on the edge.

"Mom," Lenore murmured. "I want to tell you something."

"Shhh," Mom soothed. "We'll talk later. Just sleep now."

She began smoothing back my hair and whispering, "Poor little Janine." The drone of her voice was soothing, and I remembered another day when she'd whispered that. Another day, when I was four years old and had done something terrible.

"Poor little Janine," she said. "Poor little Janine."

"Mom?" Lenore whispered. "Mother? Could you call me Lenore, just for now?" She twisted the bracelet around on my arm. Around and around and around.

Mom didn't seem surprised by her request. "Sure, honey, if it will make you feel better." Gently she rubbed my forehead. "Poor little Lenore. Poor sweet Lenore. I love you so much, Lenore."

Lenore didn't say anything more, but I could feel her relax.

Soon we were both asleep.

Dr. Zeigler was there when I woke up. She sat in a chair beside my bed. Beside *Lenore's* bed.

"Well, hello," Dr. Zeigler said when I opened my eyes.

Groggily I focused on her, wondering why

Lenore didn't swing into action immediately. Perhaps she didn't know what to say to the doctor. At any rate, I was in control again. "Hello," I said. "I didn't know doctors still made house calls."

Dr. Zeigler shrugged. "People still get sick at home." She paused to smile at me. "Your folks tell me you're having a problem."

"Did they tell you what the problem was?"

"They weren't sure they understood it. Why don't you just go ahead and tell me everything."

So I told her. I began at the beginning, with the accident, and how I found myself in that strange, beautiful place where Lenore was. I told her about returning to my body and finding Lenore there with me. I told her about Lenore's lies, and about the way she took control of me. I told her everything.

I could feel Lenore's tension as I spoke, but she made no effort to interfere or comment. Maybe she was exhausted again.

Or maybe she was just gathering strength for some new scheme.

As I spoke, Dr. Zeigler sat quietly with her palms pressed together and her index fingers against her lips. "Hmmm," she said when I finished. "So you still think Lenore came back with you there in the emergency room."

I nodded. "What shall I pack?"

"Pack?" Dr. Zeigler looked puzzled. "Pack for what?"

"I need help. Aren't you checking me into the psychiatric ward?"

Dr. Zeigler smiled a little, but her eyes were serious. "I think you'll do better at home, Janine. Now lie down and let me explain again what happened to you. We already went over this in the hospital. Remember?"

I lay back down. "I remember." She was going to pound on that multiple personality thing again.

"Now, we'll try a scenario," Dr. Zeigler said. "You've always prided yourself on your good behavior, Janine. Almost compulsive good behavior. You always did the right things. Am I on track so far?"

"Yes. Except that now and then I'd do something I didn't think was so right. Then I'd call myself Lenore."

Dr. Zeigler nodded. "On the day of the accident you felt guilty about cutting school and taking off with Scott. But he called you Lenore, so it was all right. Janine wouldn't do such a thing. Then came the accident and you got a real whack on the front of your head. When you came out of it, you found you were doing other things that Janine would not do."

She looked at me questioningly, as if to ask if I understood.

I nodded, and she went on.

"Sometimes people who have your type of injury suffer from what we call 'release of inhibition.' So to explain this straying from your usual good behavior, your subconscious mind supplied an explanation—that Lenore had come back to share your body."

It seemed to make sense. "Then it's not multiple personality?"

"I didn't say that. You supplied your own explanation, but what was happening was the fragmenting of personality. There's a lot more bothering you than just cutting school, I think."

I admitted there probably was.

"So," she said, "I'll arrange for some evaluation sessions. You'll need therapy, but I'm sure we'll be able to help you through this. Eventually your head injury will heal completely and we'll be able to integrate the two parts of your personality. That's all Lenore is, you know. She's not a separate person, Janine. That doesn't happen. She's just the other side of your own personality."

I didn't say anything.

Dr. Zeigler took my left hand and squeezed it.

"I've got some good news for you, Janine. Your former roommate, Hallie, is going to make it after all. She was so depressed for a while that we thought we might lose her."

That truly was good news. "What happened?"

Dr. Zeigler smiled. "It's odd what things will jar us loose from what's getting us down. Remember her boyfriend, Kevin?"

"I never met him."

"Neither did I. But he finally came to see Hallie one day. Came dragging in, she said, with some lame excuse about how his mother wouldn't let him visit her before that. Hallie really let him have it, I guess. Told him to go back to Mama. She's been on the mend ever since."

I laughed along with Dr. Zeigler. "Tell her I'll be in to see her soon."

Dr. Zeigler nodded. "Is there anything else I can do for you right now? Would you like a mild sedative to help you sleep tonight?"

"Yes, please," I said, like a kid wanting a lollipop.

She wrote out a prescription on a pad she pulled from the little black bag she had with her. "I'll give this to your folks and they can have it filled."

"Maybe I'll have it filled myself," I said. "Do I

have to stay in bed all day, or do you think I could go visit Scott?"

Dr. Zeigler smiled. "That's the best prescription of all, for both of you. Rest for a while, then by all means go see him, but not at the hospital. He's scheduled to come home today, you know." She walked to the door, then turned. "Scott is pretty depressed, so don't be surprised if he's a bit unresponsive. I think a visit from you might help."

"His mother called," I said. "I told her I'd visit Scott as soon as I was allowed."

"Good." Dr. Zeigler said good-bye and left.

I heard her speaking to Mom and Dad downstairs, then the front door slammed. Dad came to the bottom of the stairs to yell that whenever I was ready to go, he'd take me to see Scott. He'd be in the family room watching TV until then, he said.

I lay there trying to sort through the things Dr. Zeigler had said. I was startled when Lenore said, *"Well, well, well, isn't that interesting? When you finally decide to tell the truth, the whole truth, and nothing but the truth, the good doctor doesn't believe you."*

"What's to believe?" I said angrily. *"You heard what she said. You're not here, Lenore. You're just another part of my own personality."* I wanted to hurt her.

"*I'm here,*" she said. "*And I'm ready to prove it.*"

"*And just how do you intend to do that?*" I said defiantly even though that earlier feeling of weakness was returning.

"*I'll tell you how. Janine wants to go see Scott. Lenore wants to find Rafe and finish what they started. That's something goody-goody Janine would never do in a gazillion years. But guess where we're going.*"

I felt sick again. "*No,*" I protested, but Lenore was already swinging my legs over the side of the bed.

SIXTEEN

I couldn't stop Lenore. I thought about running to Mom and telling her to tie me to the stair railing or something. I thought about calling Dr. Zeigler and asking her to lock me in the psycho ward.

But I had no choice. Lenore was in total control.

"Turn it off," she said when I tried to tell her she couldn't go see Rafe. *"This is my day."*

Walking confidently and with surprising coordination, she took me downstairs.

Mom and Dad were in the family room watching a video, something they liked to do on holidays. William and Anna Mae were on the front porch, playing Monopoly.

Anna Mae looked closely at me. "Hi, Lenore," she said softly. "I hope you're not mad because I told."

Lenore smiled at her. "Not at all, Anna Mae. I'm glad you did. It's time everybody knows."

Anna Mae tipped her head as she watched me. "Are you going to be Lenore all the time now?"

Lenore nodded my head. "Yes. All the time." She walked me down the porch stairs. "See you guys later."

Inside my head I said, *"Which way are you going, Lenore? You don't even know where Rafe lives. It's a long way to walk."*

Lenore stopped and stood silent for a moment. Then without a word to me she turned back toward the house and went inside to the hallway where our key rack is. She took the keys to Mom's car.

"Lenore," I screamed. *"Lenore, you don't know how to drive a car."*

Lenore walked back out to the porch. *"I've watched Mom do it. I can manage."*

"Look, Lenore. If you want to talk to Rafe, let's call him on the phone."

"No," she said firmly. *"I want to be with him."*

I searched frantically for some other reason to offer. *"But you can't drive there because you still don't know where he lives."*

"And you're not going to show me?"

"No way."

Lenore looked at William and Anna Mae. "Hey,

kids," she said. "Do you know where Rafe Belmont lives?"

"Sure." William stood up. "Want me to show you?" He stood up and pointed down the street. "You go that way for a while, then you go that way and then that way." He swung his arm around.

"Why don't you come with me and show me where to turn?" Lenore said. "We'll go in the car."

William looked surprised. "I didn't know you learned how to drive."

Lenore smiled. "Janine doesn't know how, but Lenore does, William."

William's eyes got big. "Does Mom know you've got her car keys?"

"Does she have to know?" Lenore held out my hand. "Are you coming with me?"

"Yes," Anna Mae yelled. William slowly put his hand in mine.

Lenore had no problem starting the car. She backed it out of the driveway quickly in case Mom and Dad heard the engine, then headed down the street. Her handling of the car was jerky, but at least she kept it on the right side of the street.

Anna Mae took over the giving of directions. Lenore didn't look around, but I knew William was sitting silently in the backseat. I could feel his disapproval.

Calmly, Lenore followed Anna Mae's directions, turning where she told her to turn. She failed to slow down for a stop sign, but fortunately there was no cross traffic.

"This is fun," she told William and Anna Mae. "Someday soon I'll take you kids to the beach."

"Yea," Anna Mae said.

William remained silent.

Anna Mae pointed out another turn and Lenore made it, swinging wide and almost scraping the curb before she got straightened out. She giggled, then asked, "How come you kids know right where Rafe lives?"

"Everybody knows where he lives," Anna Mae said. "He wins all the football games. The girls walk past his house a lot. My sister does, and so does Janine sometimes."

"*Aha,*" Lenore said to me. "*So how come you've been telling me he isn't for me? A case of jealousy maybe, dear twin?*"

I didn't even bother to answer her. We were on Rafe's street by then anyway, and he was there in the driveway, just seating himself in his little red car.

Lenore pulled to a stop, one tire jumping up over the curb. "Rafe," she yelled. "Hi."

Rafe looked at the car, puzzled. "Hi, Janine. When did you learn to drive?"

Lenore got out of Mom's car and ran up the driveway. Opening the passenger-side door, she got in beside Rafe.

"I'm full of surprises," she said, smiling at him. "Hey, aren't you glad to see me?"

"Where are you off to?" He avoided the question.

"Here. To see you. You didn't call, so I came. By the way, I'm Lenore now. All the time."

"Yeah?" Rafe reached out to start his engine. "Well, it's good to see you, but I'm on my way to work."

"Work? Since when does a big football jock like you work?"

"Since my knee injury. I work nights and holidays at In-and-Out Burger, and I'm going to be late. See you at school." He revved the engine.

"Forget work," Lenore said. "Let's go up to your special spot. Maybe that Forest Service guy won't be around during the day."

"Sorry, Janine, not today."

"It's Lenore, Rafe. Don't you understand?"

Rafe looked straight ahead. "Okay. Lenore. I

understand. Listen, Lenore, I don't know how to say this, but I think we'd better cool it."

"Cool it?" I could tell Lenore was beginning to get the idea that something was wrong. "You mean for today. Well, how about tomorrow? I'm free anytime. Any day."

Rafe shifted uneasily in his seat. "I mean cool it for good." He gave an abrupt little laugh. "You know what my reputation is. I never hang around with one girl for very long."

"Lenore," I cried. *"Can't you understand? You're being dumped."*

Lenore shook my head. "No, not me. You can't leave me, Rafe. Not after what we had going."

"We had nothing going, Lenore."

"But I love you. I'm different from those others."

Rafe took a deep breath and turned to face me. "No. That's the problem. I thought at first you really were different, back there in the hospital room when you visited Scott. You were really sweet, except for that come-on smile. And that day at the Arboretum. That was nice, just walking around, talking and being silly. It was fun. No pressure. I don't know what's going on with you, but Janine was the one who was different."

"And Lenore?"

Rafe hesitated.

"Say it," Lenore prompted.

Rafe shrugged. "Okay, if you insist. Lenore is just like all the other girls I've been with." Opening the door, he started to get out of the car.

"Wait." Lenore grabbed hold of his arm. "No. I'm not like all the other girls. I'm better." Dragging him back into his seat, she wrapped her arms around him. "Kiss me," she whispered. "You'll remember how good it was."

He looked at me, then gently pulled away. "Good-bye, Lenore."

Lenore got out of the car, whimpering wordlessly.

Rafe closed his door, revved the engine and drove off.

I remembered Dr. Zeigler's words about how devastating rejection can be. I remembered Hallie not even wanting to live when Kevin rejected her.

With that in mind, I summoned the energy to take over. I would knock on the Belmonts' door and ask to use the telephone. I would call Mom and Dad to come get me and William and Anna Mae.

But things weren't working out that way. Lenore was angry now, and her anger made her stronger.

Running back to Mom's car, she got in and

started it, gunning the motor until it roared. Then with a squeal of tires, she lurched the car into the street, running through stop signs and careening onto busy Colorado Boulevard.

"Lenore," I screamed. "You're too upset to drive. Let me take over."

"You don't exist anymore. How could you take over? You're Lenore now." She stepped harder on the gas.

She was wrong, of course. I just could never be Lenore. Lenore did things that Janine would never do.

Or would I? Anna Mae had been right about my walking past Rafe's house. Catherine and I had done it several times, casually strolling past even though it was several blocks out of our way.

But that wasn't like actually throwing myself at him the way Lenore had done.

We swerved left onto Sierra Madre Boulevard, heading toward the intersection where Scott and I had the accident on the day we ditched school.

"Lenore." I tried to keep my voice calm. "You have to slow down. This is dangerous."

"So what? Enjoy it."

William and Anna Mae were silent in the backseat. Watching. Listening, because we were both speaking aloud now.

The light in the familiar intersection ahead was turning red. There were cars ready to start through the other way. We were going to hit somebody.

That other day came into my mind. I remembered the tearing crash. I remembered going to that place where I'd found Lenore.

Maybe this was the way to do it. The way to get rid of her. If I went back to that place now, maybe I could dump her just as surely as Rafe had done.

The car streaked on, a light rain spattering the windshield.

That day I'd been Lenore, too. Wasn't that what Scott said just before the crash? "Tell me what we should do first," he'd said. "This is your day, Lenore."

If I had been Lenore *before* the crash, then . . . then what? Then who was it I'd found among the purple mountains?

I couldn't think about it.

We were about to enter the intersection, aimed directly at a car crossing through from the left. In a few seconds it would be over, and Lenore would be delivered back to that mystical place from which she came.

"Janine!" William screamed. "Look out!"

Suddenly everything was all wrong. William and Anna Mae were not supposed to be in this scenario. What was going to happen to them?

"Lenore," I yelled. "Stop! The kids will be hurt."

Now I was Janine again. Janine would *never* endanger the little kids. Energy flowed into my arms and I was able to wrench the steering wheel to the left. We barely missed the rear of the other car, then bumped up onto the grass parkway, skidding and twisting until we came to a stop.

I turned around to see if William and Anna Mae were all right. They stared at me silently, safely held by their seat belts.

Just before other people swarmed around us from the cars that had stopped to see what was going on, Anna Mae said, "Janine, make Lenore go away."

Maybe it was Anna Mae's statement that made me remember. Or maybe it was just that I *had* to remember. I *had* to know who I really was.

At any rate, I did remember where that picture of my sister and me was.

I left the car there on the parkway strip. We'd get it later. A kind woman took me and William and Anna Mae home in her own car.

Mom and Dad weren't there. The front door was open as if they'd left in a hurry. They were probably out looking for us.

Boomer regarded me suspiciously as I walked in. He made no objection, but he didn't wag his tail, either.

In the front hall I faced Mom's big cedar chest with the mirror over it. I didn't look in the mirror. Not yet.

Opening the lid of the chest, I dug down to the very bottom. That's where I'd buried the picture after I'd cut it all those years ago. I remembered now.

The two little T-shirts, pink and blue, with the names stitched on them were there at the bottom of the chest. Folded inside each shirt was half of the photograph. I took the two halves and held them up together. I looked at Lenore, with the mole under the right side of her chin. Then at Janine with the mole under the left side of her chin.

I lifted my eyes to the mirror and stared at my own face—with the mole under the right side of my chin. The twin in the blue T-shirt—that's who I was.

That was why I'd cut the picture in two pieces all those years ago, to separate the two girls. Then I'd hidden it so I could forget what I'd discovered.

I'd been a panic-stricken seven-year-old that day. I hadn't understood exactly why I cut the picture. I'd just had a very bad feeling about it.

It was only now that I realized the truth.

The truth was that I was Lenore.

SEVENTEEN

Mom burst into the house while I stood there in front of the hallway mirror, staring into my own eyes. Staring into the eyes of Lenore.

"Thank heaven you're here," Mom cried. Her face was white and strained with anxiety, but as she came toward me it changed to red and angry. "Janine, what were you thinking? You're not qualified to drive a car alone yet. You could have killed yourself, to say nothing of William and Anna Mae."

"They're safe," I mumbled.

Mom gave a terse nod. "I saw them outside. But that's not the point. Your father is still out frantically searching for you. Janine, I can't believe you'd do such a thing." All the while she was yelling, Mom clutched my arm as if to reassure herself that I was all right.

"Janine wouldn't do such a thing, but Lenore would." I turned to look Mom squarely in the face. "Why didn't you tell me I'm Lenore?"

She blinked.

I held up the two halves of the photograph.

"Oh, you found it," she said softly. "Why, how did it get cut?"

"I cut it." I let her take the picture. "I cut it when I was seven years old. I found it one day right after you finished using it for the painting of my twin and me, and I saw that my mole was on the wrong side. It stirred up some kind of memory."

I turned away then, not wanting to look at Mom. "I was terrified that day, without understanding why," I went on. "I cut the picture, trying to separate the two of us."

I looked back to watch Mom trying to fit the two parts of the picture together. "But you know why now," she said.

"Yes." I began to tremble. "No, I'm not sure. Maybe I remember."

Mom came over to put her arm around me and guide me to the sofa in the living room. I could feel Lenore's restlessness as we sat down. No, not

Lenore's. I couldn't call her that anymore. *I* was Lenore.

Was that why she came back? To make me admit that I was Lenore? To destroy me?

"Mom," I said. "That day when Janine drowned, you said I came screaming into the house, all dripping wet and saying that Lenore had been very bad."

Mom nodded.

"What was I wearing?"

Mom's eyes seemed to unfocus as she gazed into the past. "You were wearing your little pink T-shirt and white shorts."

"The *pink* T-shirt. And which name was on the front of the shirt?"

Mom took a deep breath. "It said Janine, of course. Pink was Janine's color."

"Did you know then that I was wearing the wrong shirt?"

Mom looked down at her hands, then back at me. "Not then. The two of you were so much alike. And things were very traumatic for a while."

It was all there in my mind now, all those things I'd tried to hide from myself. I forced myself to look at them. "It was my idea to go to the pond. I was Lenore, the naughty one. Bad, bad Lenore."

210

"You *weren't* bad," Mom objected.

I went on. "We took off our shirts and shorts and waded out into the pond. When we got into trouble, I tried to help Janine, but the bottom of the pond was slippery and she kept sliding down under the water. I had no idea she was going to die. I didn't really know what death was then." To my own ears I sounded as if I were reciting a memorized script. In a way, I was. The information had been there all along, imprinted on the cells of my brain. I was merely saying what had finally risen to the surface.

"Honey," Mom said. "Are you up to this?"

"Let me finish." I took a deep, shaky breath. "I got myself out of the pond, knowing I'd be punished for the whole thing. Janine was the good one. She was never blamed for anything."

Mom was shaking her head. "Listen to me. You *were not* bad. Just a little more mischievous than your sister, but you changed after the accident. You became compulsively good."

211

"Yes, don't you see? I became Janine. The good twin. It had been Lenore's idea to go into the pond. If I was Lenore, I'd have to take the blame."

So I'd disposed of her. Got rid of her by burying that personality and becoming Janine.

As she'd said, I took her life. So where did that leave her?

Where did it leave *me*?

"I'm so sorry," I whispered. "I didn't realize."

Mom looked at me. "Didn't realize what?"

I shook my head. Mom pulled me close to her there on the sofa and stroked my back.

"We never knew if you deliberately put on Janine's shirt or if you just grabbed the first one you saw. At first we believed you really were Janine. Things were so terrible, so confusing." Mom paused, rubbing her forehead. "You insisted you were Janine, right up through your twin's burial. We put up a temporary marker with 'Lenore' on it thinking you would eventually change your mind, but you didn't."

"I remember insisting that you put Lenore on the permanent tombstone," I whispered.

And later I'd cut the picture to separate Lenore from me. I'd buried it in the chest.

"But why didn't you tell me later that I was really Lenore?" I was getting drowsy and the words came out a little mushy.

"We tried. But whenever we'd bring it up, you'd get totally hysterical, screaming that you were Janine. When we took you for therapy, you'd get into such a state that we finally abandoned it. We thought you'd remember someday, and we'd do what was necessary then. Eventually we came to know you as Janine and just let it go. We thought it didn't matter which name you were called."

"That's why you left the moles off when you did that painting, isn't it?" I mused. "I wasn't even supposed to see the photo you were working from, right? Just the painting."

"Right," Mom admitted.

My drowsiness was increasing. "Mom," I said, "Janine is here." My voice sounded far away to my own ears.

"Of course," Mom said. "You may continue to use that name if that's what you want."

"No. You don't understand. She's here with me. She came back with me when I went to that place with the crystal mountains."

"Don't talk like that."

"It's true. She's been with me since the accident. I've told you before that she was here."

Mom was rocking me a little, like a baby. "I know. But it's not possible, honey. You've just had hallucinations."

I was so drowsy that it was no trick for my twin to take over. "But it *is* possible," she said. "I'm here, Mom. I'm back. You have both of us now."

I felt Mom stiffen. Her arms loosened, and she

sat back to look at me. "I'm going to call Dr. Zei-gler." She started to get up.

"Didn't you hear me, Mommy?" my twin cried. "I'm here. Don't you want me?" She lifted my broken arm as high as she could and held out my good arm.

Mom stared at me in horror. "Stop it! Stop it! This is hideous." She stood up again and ran for the telephone.

I could feel my twin shrinking away from the hurtful words.

It was my turn again. "Mom, she *is* here." I struggled to my feet and followed Mom. "*I* wouldn't have taken the car the way Lenore did. *I* wouldn't have taken the blue bracelet. She stole it, Mom. Lenore stole it."

Then I heard what I'd just said. Lenore did all those things that I wouldn't do.

Then I had to be Janine.

No, Janine was dead. Janine, the good one.

Who was good? Who was bad? *Who was I?*

I cried to my twin. "Who am I?" I screamed aloud. "Who are *you*? Why can't you just get out!"

Mom's face was rigid as she punched numbers on the telephone. "This is Janine Palmer's mother," she cried. "I must speak to Dr. Zeigler."

Then I was running, out of the house and down the street. I could hear Mom shouting behind me.

I ran until the breath came out of me in short little gasps. I didn't know where I was going. I was just trying to get away from my twin.

I ran until I came to Scott's house. Maybe that's where I'd meant to go in the first place. To Scott, who'd always known there were two of me. Dr. Zeigler had told me he'd be coming home that day.

His mother's car wasn't in the driveway. Maybe they weren't there yet.

Stumbling up the steps, I beat on the door anyway.

"Come in," Scott called. "The door's open."

I crashed in and stood there panting by the big grandfather clock while my eyes adjusted to the dimness of the room. Scott sat on the sofa, his legs, still in casts, propped on a footstool in front of him. He faced a flickering TV set.

He stared at me, alarmed. Then he smiled and motioned for me to come to him. "I was just thinking about you. Mom's gone to get me some Chinese food, and I was wishing you were here to share it."

"Which me?" I cried. "Which one of me did you wish was here?"

"Tell him you're Lenore," my twin said. *"See if it will turn him off the way it did Rafe. TELL HIM YOU'RE LENORE."*

I felt faint, sweaty, cold. Something bonged and I wondered if I might be going off to the crystal mountains again. Or was it just the grandfather clock striking the hour?

Had the bonging always been just my memories of that clock?

A look of concern wiped away the smile on Scott's face. "What's the matter?" He dropped his arms and swung his legs from the footstool. He attempted to stand up but stumbled and collapsed on the floor, groaning. His already pale face went even whiter.

Suddenly it didn't matter who I was. I'd caused Scott to hurt himself, and that was worse than anything I'd gone through so far.

I ran to him, fighting the suffocating drowsiness that weighed me down. What was it? Was my twin trying to destroy me as I had destroyed her?

"Oh, Scotty, Scotty," I cried. "I'm sorry." I fumbled with his heavy casts, lifting his legs, helping him to get back onto the sofa. I cried when he moaned. Smoothing back his hair, I held his head against me, and then I was kissing him. *I.* Janine, Lenore, whoever *I* was.

216

Did it matter? We were both concerned about him. We both wanted to help him, comfort him.

For the first time, we blended together into one.

Scott relaxed against me. "That's the best therapy I've had yet," he whispered. "Stay with me, Janine."

I held him close for a long time, until he said his legs had stopped hurting.

Finally I straightened so I could look at him.

"Scott," I said, "I'm Lenore."

He just looked at me, putting up a hand to touch my face. "Tell me about it," he said.

I took a deep breath and told him everything.

As I did, the coldness, the faintness and drowsiness disappeared. I felt like *me* again. Whoever *me* was. Part Janine. Part Lenore. A combination of good and bad, strong and weak, light and darkness.

I would never be the same me as I'd been before.

I was sure there was a lot of therapy ahead of me. But at least now I knew that my twin, however it was that she'd returned to me, had come not to destroy but to help me face the truth.

"*Thank you,*" I whispered silently.